# The
# Thunder Keeper

# ◀ The ▶
# Thunder Keeper

## Margaret Coel

BERKLEY PRIME CRIME, NEW YORK

THE THUNDER KEEPER

A Berkley Prime Crime Book
Published by The Berkley Publishing Group,
a division of Penguin Putnam Inc.,
375 Hudson Street, New York, New York 10014.

Visit our website at
www.penguinputnam.com

First edition: September 2001

Library of Congress Cataloging-in-Publication Data

Coel, Margaret, 1937–
    The thunder keeper / by Margaret Coel.
        p. cm.
    ISBN 0-425-18188-X (alk. paper)
    1. O'Malley, John (Fictitious character)—Fiction.   2. Holden,
Vicky (Fictitious character)—Fiction.   3. Wind River Indian Reservation (Wyo.)—Fiction.   4. Catholic Church—Clergy—Fiction.
5. Arapaho Indians—Fiction.   6. Women lawyers—Fiction.
7. Wyoming—Fiction.   I. Title.

PS3553.O347 T48 2001
813'.54—dc21

                                                        00-069794

PRINTED IN THE UNITED STATES OF AMERICA

10   9   8   7   6   5   4   3   2   1

# Acknowledgments

J. David Love, Ph.D., retired research geologist, U.S. Geological Survey and acknowledged authority on the geology of Wyoming; W. Dan Hausel, senior economic geologist (metals and precious stones), Wyoming State Geological Survey, both of Laramie; Larry Loendorf, archaeologist, Durham, NC; Brad Henderson, Ph.D., satellite imaging data analyst, Boulder, CO; John Dix, former baseball player, Washington, DC; Virginia Sutter, Ph.D., member of the Arapaho tribe, Issaquah, WA; Mark Moxley, district supervisor, Lander, and Bill Hogg, inspector, Cheyenne, Wyoming Department of Environmental Quality–Land Quality Division; Swede Johnson, Jack Graves, Rebecca Fischer, and Kristin Coel Henderson, attorneys, and Sheila Carrigan, municipal court judge, Boulder; Beverly Carrigan, and Karen Gilleland, Boulder.

*My children*
*My children*
*It is I who holds the thunder in my hand*
*I show it to my children*
*I show it to my children*
*Says the Keeper*
*Says the Keeper*

In memory of
Margaret and Sam Speas
and for
Karen Gilleland
*Hohów*

# Prologue

From the ledge high on the cliff, Duncan Grover could see the length of the valley running like a river out of the mountains and into the shadows of the plains. Bear Lake directly below glistened like a diamond in the moonlight. Above the ledge, the spirit that guarded the valley had carved its own image into the flat face of the cliff. The white figure seemed to be stepping out from the reddish sandstone: large, square body with arms outstretched in a kind of benediction, and round, all-seeing eyes behind the humanlike mask.

The world was silent, except for the faint stirring of thunder beyond the mountain peaks and the sound of the wind in the junipers and piñons. The wind smelled of rain. It was the last Friday in April, the Moon of Ice Breaking in the Waters, in the way in which his people, the Arapahos, marked the passing of time.

Duncan pulled the woolen blanket tighter about his bare shoulders and sat down cross-legged inside the circle he'd drawn through the loose gravel on the ledge. He would stay inside the circle for three days, as Gus Iron Bear, the *noto'nheihi*, had instructed. Here was everything he needed for his vision quest: a small fire of cottonwood chips, and sage, a pipe carefully wrapped in calico and propped on two upright sticks, and a leather pouch filled with tobacco.

He tried not to think about the hunger gnawing at his insides like a small animal. His mouth was as dry as leather. He hadn't eaten or taken anything to drink for two days now, he guessed. He couldn't be sure. All of time had collapsed into the present.

He intended to follow the medicine man's instructions to the last detail. He didn't want to fail. He'd already failed so many life tests that he felt himself a mighty failure. But he'd been given another chance.

He'd spent three weeks preparing for the vision quest: days and nights of praying, fasting, and listening to the words of the *noto'nheihi*. He'd been cleansed in the sweat lodge, his heart softened so that it might be reshaped by the spirits. He'd prayed for strength, for the power to control his emotions throughout the ordeal of the quest, like a warrior seeking the power to control himself throughout the ordeal of battle.

Two days ago he'd driven thirty miles north of the Wind River Reservation to Bear Lake Valley. The spirits dwelled in the valley, and had dwelled there for countless old men, countless generations—as long as his people could remember. He'd removed his clothes and slipped past the icy crust still clinging to Bear Lake, surprised at how warm the water was, how comforting as it lapped at his nakedness and cleansed his spirit.

Then he'd wrapped himself in the blanket woven with blue, red, and yellow geometric symbols: the long lines that represented the roads humans must follow, the circle that represented the Creator, the center of all. Carrying only a small bundle that contained the pipe, the pouch, and some cottonwood chips and dried sage, he'd climbed up the mountain barefoot. Floated upward, it had seemed, lifted into the sky by the spirit itself looming above, the rocks and pine needles as nothing beneath his feet. He found the ledge with no trouble. It was much larger than he'd expected, as large as a porch. It might have been waiting for him through the eons.

With his fingers he'd traced out the circle, his home on the ledge, then removed the pipe from the bundle and tapped in the tobacco. Before he began to smoke, he held out the pipe to the four directions, an offering to the four grandfather spirits that guarded the world. When he offered the pipe to the spirit of the west, the thunder keeper had answered. Thunder, *boh'o:o,* had crashed through the valley.

He'd waited for the thunder to subside before he'd turned to the sandstone cliff and raised the pipe to the figure of the guardian spirit of the valley.

"Remember me." He spoke softly to the spirit. "I am poor. Every morning I will be poor. Take pity on me."

Only after he'd made the offerings did he begin to smoke. The smoke had curled up toward the sky, lifting his prayers to the spirits. A sense of peace had come over him. He felt strong with confidence that the spirits would honor his quest.

Since then he'd dozed inside the circle, then awakened and prayed and smoked before dozing again, waiting—not expecting, simply waiting—for the time his guardian spirit might choose to come in a vision and bestow power upon him. To receive power in a vision—ah, that would be the strongest power of all. Then he would have the strength to follow the Arapaho Way. He could live a good life.

He wasn't sure when he became aware of the light flowing through the trees on the mountainside below, but now it caught his attention. Be attentive to all things—

the *noto'nheihi*'s voice in his head. He tried to concentrate on the moving light, emptying his mind of all other thoughts and possibilities. He felt his heart knocking against his ribs. He struggled to take in a deep breath and calm himself. He must be ready. The spirit was approaching.

# ❮ 1 ❯

Rain scattered like shotgun pellets over the roof of St. Francis Church. From the distance came the sound of thunder, diffused and muted. Every time the front door opened, a blast of cool, moist air rattled the door to the confessional and swept through the cracks into the small cubicle.

Father John O'Malley slipped a bookmark between the pages of *Indian Country* and flexed his long legs into the shadows beyond the tiny circle of light from the lamp behind his chair. The rungs of the wooden chair dug into his back muscles. He should move one of the upholstered chairs from his office to the confessional, he reminded himself. The trouble was, he always forgot until the next time he heard confessions.

Just inside the door was another straight-back chair, so close he could shove it sideways with his boot. There was always a penitent who preferred the informality of talking to the priest face-to-face in the sacrament of reconciliation, but most of his parishioners liked the traditional anonymity of the confessional, whispering sins and failings, remorse and prayers from the tiny cubicle on the other side of the metal grate in the paneled wall to his left. Arapahos were traditional.

He glanced at his watch. Almost four-thirty. He'd been in the confessional since three. Every Saturday afternoon, between three and four-thirty, either he or whatever assistant priest happened to be assigned to St. Francis Mission on the Wind River Reservation could be found in the confessional. Usually they took turns. Today had been the turn of his new assistant, Father Don Ryan, but something had come up. Father Don had to go out. Could Father John possibly hear confessions?

It had been fifteen minutes since the last penitent. Father John stood up and stamped his boots on the thin carpet, trying to work the stiffness out of his legs. He was about to shrug into the jacket that he'd draped over the back of his chair when he heard the front door open. A stream of chilled air filtered into the confessional.

He sat back down.

Finally the door on the other side of the confessional opened, and a slim dark shadow slid across the grate. There was a noisy intake of breath, then another.

Father John felt his senses switch to alert, the way they had when he was a kid back in Boston, coming home from baseball practice after dark, spotting a gang of tough older boys under the street lamp down the block.

He said, "Do you wish to make a confession?"

"Yeah, I wanna confess." A man's voice, the slightest midwestern accent. The man was not Arapaho.

"Please begin." Father John bent his head toward the grate. In the dim patchwork of light, he could make out the protruding nose, the hooded eyes. The rest of the face was lost in shadow.

"I gotta tell somebody what happened." The man spoke hurriedly. "But it's gotta be, what d'ya call it, confidential. Know what I mean? I remembered going to confession when I was a kid, so I come here. You aren't gonna go blabbing, are you?"

For a moment Father John considered explaining the conditions required for a valid sacrament—intent to confess, sincere remorse, firm purpose of amending one's life—then thought better of it. The man was here, and he needed to confess.

He said, "Whatever you say in the confessional stays in the confessional."

A long sigh, a mixture of relief and impatience, burst through the grate, leaving an aftermath of garlic and mint.

"I didn't mean for the Indian to get killed—"

"What Indian?" Father John interrupted.

"Up there on the ledge, watching. I didn't think the boss was gonna kill him."

"What are you talking about?" Father John leaned forward, all of his senses alert. He could feel his skin prickling. The air was heavy around him, the sound of the rain far away.

"I'm trying to tell you, Father." Impatience leaked through the voice. "Me and the boss went up the mountain to talk to the Indian. At least that's what I thought was gonna happen. Encourage him to mind his own business. Maybe punish him a little, know what I mean? The boss likes that. The Indian looked like he was strung out on dope. Sitting cross-legged like a beggar, his eyes glazed over. He was just staring up at the carving in the rock. Next thing I know, the boss hits him in the head with a pipe. Christ, I didn't even know the boss was carrying a pipe. Then he picks up the Indian like a sack of garbage and tosses him over the cliff." The voice had begun to crack, remorse and despair leaking through.

Father John was quiet. He was trying to get his mind around what the man had said. There had been a murder.

An Indian thrown off a cliff. A couple of seconds passed before he was aware that the man in the shadows was waiting for him to say something.

"Did you go to the police?" he managed.

The man spit out a laugh, and the odor of garlic was so strong that Father John held his breath a moment. "You think I wanna be the next guy thrown off a cliff? The boss finds out I opened my mouth, I'm gonna be a dead man."

"You witnessed a murder," Father John said. "You have an obligation before God. You must try to make some amends. Whoever did this must be brought to justice."

"Let me tell you about justice." There was another forced laugh, another cloud of garlic. "I go to the police and I die. That's justice. Soon's I get what's owed me, I'm getting away from here. I don't want no part of any more murders."

"More murders! What are you saying?"

"The boss is mopping up. He's gonna kill anybody gets in the way. The Indian was just the first. There's gonna be more murders."

"Listen to me." Father John kept his own voice low and firm. "The police—"

"Forget it, Father. I come here for confession, not some high-and-mighty lecture. I'm not going to the police."

Suddenly the atmosphere changed, as if new air had rushed in to fill a vacuum, and Father John realized the man was getting to his feet: the protruding nose and hooded eyes rising upward into the shadows.

"Don't go," he said, but the door on the other side was already open, the crack of light illuminating the thin figure in a red baseball jacket and blue jeans. For half a second light glinted on the bald head. The door slammed shut. There was the *tap-tap* sound of footsteps hurrying away.

"Wait!" Father John was on his feet, knocking the other chair into the wall. His jacket and book fell to the floor. He flung open the door and crossed the vestibule. No sign of the man.

He swung around and walked through the open doors to the main part of the church, his eyes searching the center aisle, the silent rows of pews, the altar. A red votive candle in front of the tabernacle on the left side of the altar blinked little circles of light over the ceiling. The church was empty.

He retraced his steps through the vestibule, past the confessional, to the front door. The knob was still moist with perspiration as he yanked the door open and stepped onto the concrete stoop.

"Wait!" he shouted into the rain beating down on the mission grounds, running in little streams across Circle Drive. The administration building, the Arapaho Museum, the priest's residence along Circle Drive rose out of the rainy haze like ships tossing in the sea. The only vehicles were his old red Toyota pickup and Father Don's blue sedan parked in front of the residence. There was no one around.

Father John hunched his shoulders against the rain and ran down the alley that divided the church from the administration building. Past Eagle Hall. Past the guest house, the rain plastering his shirt to his back and chest. He blinked the water out of his eyes. Still no sign of anyone, no footprints in the muddy alley. The man had evaporated into the rain, like a spirit.

Unless . . . unless he hadn't left the church after all. Unless he was still inside.

# ◄ 2 ►

Father John whirled about and ran back to the church. He walked slowly down the aisle, checking each pew. Then he crossed the altar to the sacristy, checking the corners, the shadows, half expecting some specter to rise up before him or emerge from the closet where he kept the Mass vestments. The sacristy was empty.

He made his way back to the confessional and looked in the penitent's side. The faint odor of sweat and nervousness and garlic permeated the small space. He went around to his own side and grabbed his jacket, then turned off the lights.

Outside on the stoop, he pulled the jacket over his wet shirt, which clung to his shoulders and arms like a new skin, and peered into the rain. It was then that he saw the red taillight flickering like a firefly through the cottonwoods that lined the straightaway out to Seventeen Mile Road. In a moment the taillight was gone.

Father John plunged across Circle Drive, through the field of wet grass, trying to avoid the gathering pools of water. His mind replayed the man's confession, stopping at the same places, like a needle sticking in the same grooves in the opera records his father used to play. *The Indian was the first. There's gonna be more murders.*

There hadn't been any deaths on the reservation lately, not since Josephine Matley had died peacefully in her bed at age ninety-six. He and Father Don had said the funeral Mass together. A warm, sunny spring day. The church had been packed, and people had to stand outside, listening to the sermon through the open windows. No one had died since then—two weeks ago yesterday. As far as he knew.

He let himself in the front door, nearly colliding with Father Don. Obviously on his way out: long black raincoat, safari-type hat tilted slightly on his head. The new assistant was still in his thirties, a Jesuit for only a few years. A good-looking guy, Father John supposed, with sandy-colored hair, pale gray eyes lit with amusement and curiosity, a quick smile. He was about six feet tall—a few inches shorter than Father John—with a lanky, athletic frame and relaxed posture that seemed permanent, as if the man couldn't imagine a situation in which he wouldn't be at ease.

Two months ago he'd been teaching mathematics in a Jesuit prep school in Milwaukee. After the last assistant, Father Kevin McBride, had returned to Marquette University to teach anthropology, and after Father John had called the Provincial three, four, six times, pleading for help, and the Provincial had gotten good and tired of taking his calls, Father Don Ryan had arrived.

"Have a minute?" Father John said, hanging his jacket over the coattree. The smell of wet wool mingled with the odor of chilis, onions, and seared meat that drifted down the hallway from the kitchen. A cabinet door slammed shut, and there was the noise of water gushing into the sink. Elena, the housekeeper, was still here. And Walks-On, the golden retriever he'd found in the ditch a couple of years ago, padded down the hall on his three legs and stuck a cold nose into the palm of his hand.

"Well, I'm on my way out . . ." The other priest made an exaggerated motion of pulling back the sleeve of his raincoat and peering at his watch. "A minute." He seemed to consider this. "Sure, why not."

Father John patted the dog's head, then walked into the study, flipping on the wall switch as he went. A white light flooded over the twin wingback chairs that he kept for visitors, the bookcases along the walls, the desk with papers spilling over the top. He dropped onto the leather chair behind the desk. His shirt felt cold and clammy against his back.

Father Don was standing just inside the door, leaning against the frame, arms folded across the front of his raincoat. "Shoot," he said.

"Confessions today . . ." Father John began.

The other priest walked over and sat down in the chair across from the desk. He leaned forward. "Somebody came to the confessional and told you something that you don't want to know. Am I right?" Concern worked through his voice.

Father John nodded.

"That's tough, John, but you can't repeat what you heard." The man's pale eyes darkened like the thunderclouds outside. "We're bound by the seal of the confessional, two thousand years old. You can't break it."

"Suppose someone were to die."

Father Don took a few moments. Then, as if he'd come to a decision, he said, "We're speaking hypothetically, right? Did the penitent give you any details? Did he say someone in particular was in danger? Is there anything a hypothetical priest could do to prevent a death?"

Father John shook his head.

The other priest shrugged and pushed to his feet. "Well,

there you are. You can't be blamed for keeping the information to yourself. If you knew somebody was in danger, you might have to find some way to warn him. Fact is, you don't know." He started moving to the entry, rechecking his watch. "I really have to go. I'd like to invite you along, but"—he jammed both hands into his coat pockets—"I'm having dinner with a friend."

Father John waved away the explanation, and the other priest disappeared into the entry. The sound of the front door shutting was like a clap of thunder that rippled through the floorboards of the old house.

His assistant was right, Father John thought. Every instinct, every sense of logic, told him so, and yet . . . *There's gonna be more murders.* The words kept running through his mind.

He got up and walked over to the stack of *Gazettes* on the table beneath the window and began scanning today's paper for an article on a body found in the mountains. He'd glanced through the paper this morning; he hadn't seen anything, but there could have been a small article, easy to miss. There was nothing. He thumbed through yesterday's paper, the previous day's, working his way back through the week. He was halfway through the stack when he felt another presence in the room, a pair of eyes boring into his back.

He glanced around. Elena, the housekeeper, stood in the doorway, hands on her waist in a perfect imitation of his own mother at the end of her wits with the redheaded, stubborn, analytical kid who was her son. The image made him smile. Elena was probably seventy, although she claimed to have lost track of her age years ago. Old enough, she would say, for eight kids, seventeen grandkids, four great-grandkids. She knew all the names and birth dates and there were times when she insisted upon listing them for him. The family was half-Arapaho, half-Cheyenne, or Shyela, as the Arapahos called the tribe they had lived with on the plains in the Old Time, and she'd managed them all as well as the succession of priests at St. Francis Mission for years now—exactly how many years was also a figure she claimed to have forgotten.

"Your supper's waiting," she announced, bending her head sideways and wiping both hands on the white apron tied around her waist. The light glinted through her tightly curled gray hair.

"I'm coming," he said.

"Yeah? Well, so's Christmas."

He had to laugh. He could almost hear his mother's voice.

She said, "The chili's gonna be cold before you get yourself to the kitchen."

He tossed aside the last newspaper—nothing about a murdered man—and followed her down the hallway to the kitchen. She walked with shoulders squared, elbows at her sides pumping back and forth, propelling the short, stout body forward.

"Sit down," she ordered, and he took his usual chair at the round oak table. Walks-On was snoring on his blanket in the corner. The smell of chili made Father John realize how hungry he was. Elena ladled the thick soup into a bowl and set it in front of him. He took a spoonful, savoring the spicy warmth that settled in his stomach, his thoughts still on what he'd heard in the confessional.

"I said it's a shame." Elena set a plate of bread and a mug of coffee next to his bowl, and he realized her voice had been droning in the background and he had no idea what she'd been telling him.

"You eatin' supper all alone again," she said. "Nobody here but the dog."

He made an effort to give her his attention. "Why don't you join me?"

"I was just sayin' how it's Saturday night, and my granddaughter Elsie is bringing the babies, Nathan and Jordan, over for a visit. And besides, I gotta finish some beading for the arts-and-crafts fair tomorrow, so I gotta get home." She turned back to the stove and began pouring the chili into a refrigerator bowl. "Enough chili here to feed a horse," she went on, making a clucking noise, "and Father Don out to dinner."

"You're saying the man eats like a horse?" Father John took another spoonful.

"Out last night and the night before. Going here, going there. Visiting folks all over the res. The man doesn't have the sense to stay home."

"He's a popular fellow," Father John said absentmindedly. He was thinking that the Indian's body hadn't been found yet. It was somewhere on a mountainside. It could be weeks or months before some hiker spotted it. Precious time in which others could die.

"You ask me, he's gonna be gone permanently."

"What?" Father John tried to catch up.

Elena leaned toward him, both hands flattened on the table. "Father Don. You mark my words. He'll be leaving here soon."

She had his full attention now. What she said surprised him. Father Don seemed to have taken to the job here. Chatting with Elena in the kitchen over mugs of coffee, trailing Leonard, the caretaker, over the grounds, asking questions about trimming trees and touching up the paint and probably a lot of other things that, Father John suspected, he didn't really care about. He'd taken over the education committee, the liturgy committee. He was handling the mission finances. A mathematician. The man actually liked handling the finances.

He said, "What makes you think Father Don's going anywhere?"

"He's got that look in his eye." Elena whirled around and began running a dishcloth over the edge of the sink. "You know what I mean." She draped the cloth on the faucet, untied the white apron, and folded it on the counter. "When he don't know you're watching, he stares out at the plains. He sees someplace far away. That's where he's gonna go." She spread her hands wide, as if there was no help for it, and started down the hallway.

Father John scooped the last of the chili from the bowl and took a bite of bread. Less than an hour before, Father Don had been in the study, listening intently. Then he'd seemed to shift gears, his attention on the evening ahead, the dinner he was off to. Elena could be right. Father John hated to admit it. The prospect of pleading with the Provincial again for a new assistant filled him with dread.

"There's fried chicken in the fridge for your supper tomorrow." The housekeeper was back in the doorway, her dark raincoat buttoned tight across her chest, fingers tying a plastic hood over her gray hair. She always prepared chicken for Sunday dinner. A habit he'd gotten so used to, he figured that for the rest of his life he'd expect to eat cold fried chicken on Sundays.

"Before you go, Elena," he said, getting to his feet, "have you heard of anybody on the res who might be missing?"

She stared up at him, eyes widening with understanding. "So that's what's on your mind. Somebody's gone missing. Who is it?"

"I was hoping you could tell me."

"I don't know everything that's going on around here."

He doubted that was true. Elena seemed to have a direct connection to the moccasin telegraph. She always had the news hours, sometimes days, before he heard it. Strange that something about the murdered Indian hadn't flashed over the telegraph.

"Soon's I hear anything, I'll let you know." Elena gave him a wave and turned down the hallway. In a moment the front door opened and shut, sending a wave of moist air floating into the kitchen.

Father John washed out his bowl, set it on the drain, and walked back to his study. His desk was piled with matters awaiting his attention. Letters to answer. Phone calls to return. He sank down into the old leather chair, pushed the papers aside, and wished—the trace of a wish that came on him when he least expected it—that he had a sip of whiskey. A sip or two would clear his mind.

He forced his mind back to the murdered Indian. Maybe somebody had only reported him missing this afternoon and the news hadn't gotten to the moccasin telegraph yet. The police could have already found the body. And if that was the case, a murder investigation would be under way. The authorities would warn anybody else who might be in danger and . . . He drew in a long breath. He could sleep peacefully tonight.

He picked up the phone and dialed the number for the Wind River police. Within a couple of minutes, he was patched through to the home of Chief Art Banner, and the man was crackling over the line about how he was off duty and how this had better be an emergency.

"Look, Banner," Father John began, "I'm wondering if anybody was reported missing today."

"Missing?" A long whistle sounded at the other end. "You trying to ruin the first peaceful Saturday night I've had in months, O'Malley? What're you talking about?"

"Somebody who might have disappeared . . ." He selected his words carefully.

"What d'ya know that I oughta know?"

"Look, Banner, I'm just asking if anyone filed a missing person's report."

"You heard some rumors, that it?"

Father John didn't say anything.

"There's always rumors floating around the res, John, but nobody's come in to make a report in the last month. That satisfy you? I got Sherlock Holmes on TV."

Father John told the chief to go back to his mystery, then he set the receiver in the cradle. There were people walking around this evening, settling down to a pizza maybe, watching TV, who were about to be killed. A man had already been killed. An Indian. Sooner or later somebody on the res was bound to start asking questions.

He planned to visit the arts-and-crafts fair tomorrow anyway. Now he thought the fair would be a good opportunity to catch up with the latest news on the moccasin telegraph.

# ❰ 3 ❱

reat Plains Hall rose out of the prairie ahead. Father John had heard the drums as soon as he'd come around the bend on Seventeen Mile Road. The rhythmic thuds reverberated through the sounds of "Quando me'n vo" coming from the tape player wedged in the front seat of the Toyota pickup. The thuds grew stronger. He reached down and pressed the off button, allowing the beat of the drums to fill up the cab.

On the horizon, the Wind River mountains, azure blue and green with the recent rains, poked into the clouds, but patches of sunshine lay over the flat, open plains that ran into the distances on either side of the road. The air was cool, tinged with both the coming warmth of summer and the promise of more rain.

Father John made a right turn onto the dirt road that ran past the senior citizens' center to Great Plains Hall. The field in front was filled with vehicles parked at odd angles. Old trucks and pickups next to shiny SUVs and sedans. The Arapaho arts-and-crafts fair always drew a mixture of Indians from the res and white people from the adjacent towns of Riverton and Lander.

He parked next to a brown pickup as rusted and dented as the Toyota and made his way around the vehicles toward the hall, his boots sinking into the soggy ground. The faintest roll of thunder in the distance mingled with the sound of the drums.

The hall was packed, and a crowd of brown and white faces moved along the tables that had been arranged against the side walls. He could see the jewelry on the table just inside the door—beaded necklaces, bracelets, earrings: a white woman holding up a hand mirror and staring at the beaded earrings that dangled from her ears, nodding to the grandmother behind the table, handing the old woman a few bills.

Across the hall, the drummers and singers sat huddled around a large drum. The steady thuds bounced off the cement walls, punctuating the hum of voices. A group of kids dressed in dance regalia was lining up alongside the musicians, their shiny shirts and dresses, feathered headdresses, and bustles flashing through the crowd.

The smells of fresh coffee and fried bread permeated the air. In the far corner was the food table, and Father John caught sight of his assistant, Father Don, chatting with several Arapahos, tilting his head sideways—that way of his when he was listening—sipping from a Styrofoam cup, then throwing his head back and laughing. Other Indians started crowding around. The man seemed completely at ease, as if this was home. Elena could be wrong. Father John hoped so. People here liked the new assistant, and he liked them. The man was good with people.

Father John started along the tables, stopping to chat with the Arapahos seated on folding chairs on the other side. Old people, kids, men and women in their twenties and thirties—the artists and craftspeople who had beaded the jewelry and vests, painted the shirts and dresses and small drums, sewn the Arapaho star quilts, and fashioned the bows and arrows and coup sticks, just as their grand-parents had done in the Old Time.

On one table were several oil paintings that captured the beauty and loneliness of the plains and the hidden valleys of the Wind River mountains. As beautiful as any paintings of the area he'd seen. He gave a thumbs-up to Stone Yellowman, the young man watching him from the other side of the table, and the brown face broke into a wide, reassured grin.

He turned toward the next table, then stopped. For an instant he'd thought Vicky Holden was across the hall: the slim figure and shoulder-length black hair, the finely sculptured brown face, the shining, intelligent black eyes. A woman who resembled her, that was all, and he realized he'd been half expecting to see Vicky here. She wouldn't have missed the arts-and-crafts fair if she still lived in the area.

He shook away the sense of loss that came over him at the most unexpected moments. Vicky Holden had gone back to work at her old law firm in Denver five months ago. It was the way it should be. Still, he missed their friendship, missed working with her—lawyer and priest: they'd been a good team—missed being able to pick up the phone and run something by her, test some far-fetched theory against the toughness of her mind. He could have talked to her about a missing Indian.

"Father John, over here."

He swung around. Louise Little Horse was getting to her feet, beckoning him toward her table.

"How are you, Grandmother?" he said, walking over.

The old woman picked up a bolo tie and held it out in her small pink palm. The round disk was covered with tightly woven white beads. In the center—it might have been soaring through the clouds—was the blue-beaded figure of a thunderbird, the symbol of thunder, the guardian of the atmosphere. Radiating out from the bird figure were red lines, symbolizing the sun and life.

"It's beautiful," he said.

"I made it for you." She looked up at him, the narrow, dark eyes shining in the furrowed face.

"Please let me pay you for it," he said, fishing in his jeans pocket for some bills.

"Oh, no." An aggrieved look came into the dark face. She reached out, took his hand, and folded his fingers around the tie, and he thought of what the elders always said: accept the gifts offered you and be grateful.

"Thank you, Grandmother." He slipped the beaded rope around his neck and pulled the disk up under the collar of his shirt. "I'll wear it with pride," he told her.

"It'll protect you," she said. Then: "You look real Arapaho now. Only you gotta grow black hair."

"I hear there's other ways."

"I hear shoe polish works."

He laughed.

"What's worrying you, Father?" The old woman leaned across the table.

"It shows?"

She nodded.

"Tell me, Grandmother," he began. "Any news on the moccasin telegraph that the pastor at St. Francis hasn't heard yet?"

Now it was her turn to laugh. The brown face crinkled into the lines that fanned from her eyes and mouth. "Oh, I'd say there's always something that folks'd just as soon the pastor didn't know about."

"Have you heard that anybody's missing?"

She nodded.

He remained still. The pounding drums, the hum of

voices receded around them. Finally she said, "Warriors went out today looking for somebody. Ben Holden . . ."

"Ben Holden." He repeated the name, almost to himself. First the face in the crowd, now the mention of Vicky's ex-husband. The reminders brought little stabs of pain that he tried to push away.

". . . called my grandson real early. Five A.M. Woke up the whole house. Said somebody got lost up at Bear Lake. My grandson took off. They was gonna start lookin' soon's it got light."

"Who, Grandmother? Who were they looking for?" Father John kept his eyes on the old woman's. A name. He needed a name. Then he could go to the family. He could find out who else might be in danger and he'd find some way—there had to be a way—to warn them.

The old woman was shaking her head. "Soon's I find out—" The drums stopped, and silence poured over the crowd. There was a screech of a microphone.

"Welcome to the Arapaho spring arts-and-crafts fair." An Indian in blue jeans and a red western shirt, a cowboy hat pushed back on his head, strode into the center of the hall, trailing the mike cord across the tiled floor. He rattled off a string of names, thanking the elders and grandmothers for their hard work so that folks could buy traditional Arapaho art for their homes. "Let's give a big hand"—he raised one hand in the air—"for the kids from Arapaho school that are gonna demonstrate the traditional dances."

The crowd began to cheer as the drums started up. The high-pitched voices of the singers floated above the thud. Slowly the line of kids moved into the center of the hall, moccasined feet tapping in precise steps. They wore tanned hide dresses and shirts decorated with tiny tin bells that jangled as they danced. The boys held staffs, the girls, elaborate fans made of feathers.

As Father John stepped back to let the kids pass, he saw the bulky, dark figure of Chief Banner framed in the entrance. The chief gestured with his head toward the outdoors, then backed away. Father John waited for the last kid to dance past before he went outside.

Banner was standing next to a white police car parked in front of the hall, hands jammed into the pockets of his navy-blue uniform jacket. The silver insignias on his collar and cap glinted in the sunshine.

"I figured you'd be here," he said as Father John approached. "You gotta tell me everything you know about the missing Indian."

"You found him?"

The chief gave a quick nod. "Ben Holden took a half-dozen warriors up to Bear Lake this morning after the guy didn't get back from a vision quest. Found his body in a boulder field below the spirit cliff. Looks like he's been dead a couple days."

"Who is he?"

"Nobody from around here. Arapaho from Oklahoma. Name's Duncan Grover. Age about twenty-five." The chief glanced away a moment. "Fremont County Sheriff's Department brought the body out. This is their investigation, with Bear Lake being county land. Got a detective on it named Matt Slinger."

Father John understood. There was a jurisdictional maze that the law enforcement agencies in the area had to navigate. Who was in charge depended upon where a crime took place.

"What do you know about Duncan Grover, John?" The chief's eyes bore into his.

"Look, Banner," Father John began, "this isn't something I can talk about."

Banner moved closer. The odor of stale coffee hung

between them. "You do know what really happened up there, don't you?"

"What does the detective say happened?"

"The detective? You wanna know what the white detective and the white coroner say? They say Duncan Grover jumped off the cliff. Committed suicide."

"Suicide!" Father John could feel his heart speed up. He turned away a moment. They had it all wrong. The killer was going to walk away, and other people were going to die. *There's gonna be more murders.*

He looked back at the Indian watching him with narrowed eyes. "What makes them think it was suicide?"

"Body was two hundred feet below the ledge," the chief said. "If he'd accidentally stepped off, he probably wouldn't have fallen more than ten, fifteen feet before he would've been stopped by a big outcropping. But he flew over the outcropping, which took some force. They say he jumped."

"And you don't think so," Father John said after a moment.

"I don't think any warrior's gonna go on a vision quest at a sacred site like Bear Lake, where the spirits are all around, then throw himself off the cliffs." Banner's voice was tight with fury.

Father John was quiet a moment. "You explain that to the detective?"

"Yeah." The chief threw his head back in a nod. "So did Gus Iron Bear, the medicine man that gave Grover instructions. So did Holden. Three Indians explaining how things are to white men. You think they listened? Case closed, as far as they're concerned. Just another dead Indian who killed himself."

"There has to be some evidence at Bear Lake." Father John pushed on, struggling to find another way to the truth, groping toward the logic. "Footprints or tire tracks. Something that would make the detective and coroner change their minds."

"You forget it's been raining all week." A look of exasperation came into the Indian's dark eyes. "The searchers and sheriff's boys were up there trampling around all morning. If there was any evidence, it's gone." He nodded toward the sound of the drums, the jangling of the dancers who spilled out of the hall. "Those kids in there, they're gonna hear suicide and they're gonna think, warrior offs himself, so it must be okay. Goin' gets tough, and it's the way out."

The chief came closer still and took hold of his arm. Father John could feel the anger pulsing through the man's fingers. "You know the truth, John. What're you gonna do about it?"

Father John didn't say anything. The penitent's words— *more murders, more murders*—boomed silently in his head.

The chief whirled about and started around the car, and Father John felt as if a door had slammed between them, and something was drawing to a close, a friendship ending, the trust people here had in him fading away. He said, "I'll have a talk with the detective."

Banner stopped and stared at him over the roof of the car. "What're you gonna say that'll make any difference?"

He didn't know. But he knew how white men thought. It didn't surprise him that they'd ignored what the Indians had tried to tell them about spirits and vision quests. The detective and coroner would want concrete facts and logic, a straight, uncluttered path to the truth. He was like them. Somehow he was going to have to get the kind of facts that would convince them that Duncan Grover had not committed suicide.

"I'll think of something," he said. He started toward the parking lot, then walked back. The chief was behind the steering wheel, turning the ignition. The engine rumbled into life.

"What's Ben Holden got to do with this?" Father John leaned toward the driver's window rolled halfway down.

"Holden and Grover's dad were army buddies," Banner said over the top of the glass. "Soon's the kid got to the res, he went out to the Arapaho Ranch to see Holden about a job."

Father John thumped the rear door with his fist as the car started sliding by. He watched as the chief made a turn around the last row of parked vehicles and gunned the engine past the senior center and out onto Seventeen Mile Road.

Before he went to see a white man by the name of Detective Matt Slinger, he'd find out what Ben Holden knew about Duncan Grover.

# ‹ 4 ›

It took Father John almost an hour to drive north to Thermopolis, another hour heading west into the Owl Creek Mountains. A rainy haze lay over the piñons and junipers passing outside the windows. The sounds of *La Bohème* rose above the hum of the tires on wet asphalt. He spotted the turn into the Arapaho Ranch ahead, eased on the brake pedal, and made a sharp right onto the gravel road that dead-ended at a two-story log building. The smell of wet sage and new grasses hit him as he walked up to the wide porch along the front of the building and knocked on the door. There were no sounds except for that of water washing out of a downspout and the aluminum chairs banging against the porch railing in the wind.

He knocked again, then tried the knob. It turned in his hand, and he stepped into a cavernous room with overstuffed sofas and chairs and Indian rugs scattered about the plank floor. On the right was the kitchen with U-shaped cabinets that wrapped around a long, narrow table with chairs pushed into the sides. Ahead, a stairway rose to a second-floor balcony that overlooked the living room. Beyond the railing were closed doors that Father John guessed led to the bunk rooms.

"Hello!" he called. "Anybody here?"

One of the doors opened. An Indian who looked about sixty, dressed in blue jeans and plaid shirt, sauntered over to the railing. "You lookin' for somebody?"

"Ben Holden around?"

The Indian gestured with his head toward the window at the end of the balcony. "Out in the barn. Loadin' up hay for the back pasture."

"Thanks." Father John tipped the brim of his cowboy hat and stepped back outside. Hunching his shoulders in the rain, he walked down the driveway past a series of outbuildings just as a group of cowboys emerged through the side door of a barn streaked yellow with age. He spotted Ben Holden at once: the tall frame slightly stooped inside the black slicker, the black cowboy hat tilted low over his forehead.

The Indian glanced around. Then he started toward him. "What can I do for you?" His tone was businesslike, the dark eyes that regarded him steady and unreadable.

Father John felt a pang of admiration at Ben Holden's control, more certain than his own. There was a lot of history between them; they cared about the same woman, but not well enough, either of them. Ben—in and out of rehab, a violent drunk; and he, a priest.

He said, "I'd like to talk to you."

Ben gave a noncommittal shrug and veered along a diagonal path to a shack. "In here," he called, throwing his voice over one shoulder and opening the door.

Father John followed him into the small room jammed with a table and two chairs. Stacks of paper covered the tabletop and crept onto the chairs and then onto the floor. A potbelly stove hissed in the corner. The air felt warm and close.

Ben pushed a chair back with a muddy boot, lifted

some papers onto the table, and sat down. He unsnapped his slicker but made no effort to remove it, a sign that the conversation would be short.

"This about Vicky?" he said, a hard edge in his tone.

Father John cleared a stack from the other chair, swung it around, and straddled it, facing the Indian. "No," he said.

A mixture of barely concealed relief and curiosity came into the man's dark eyes. His whole frame seemed to relax against the rungs of his chair. "I get it," he said. "You're here about Duncan Grover."

"I understand you knew him."

Ben shifted sideways, stretched out his legs, and crossed one muddy boot over the other. "Duncan's dad and I were stationed in Germany together. The only Indians in the whole country"—he stared across the room at the memory—"couple Arapahos. Grover was from Oklahoma. His kid showed up at the res last month and looked me up. Said he'd been working in Denver and had enough of white people." Ben gave a snort of laughter.

"Did he say where he'd been working?" Father John asked.

"Construction jobs. Looked like he was used to hard work, mostly outdoors." He paused. The fire hissed into the quiet. "Nervous kid, looking over his shoulder all the time, like he expected an evil spirit to jump out at him. I figured he was on the run. Took a bad road in the city, came to the res to hide out and start over. I've started over a few times myself." He glanced away again. "Anyway, the kid needed a job. I told him to come back in a couple weeks when we started moving the herd to the upper pastures, and I'd take him on."

Father John didn't say anything for a moment. "What was he running from?"

"I didn't push him. He was serious about starting over, that's all I cared about. Told him to go see Gus Iron Bear so he could get back on the Arapaho road. He took instructions from the old man, then went up to Bear Lake for his vision quest. When he didn't come back, Gus asked me to take some of the skins and go looking for him."

Ben pulled in his long legs and leaned over the table. "Detective Slinger and the coroner say Grover killed himself. What a load of bullshit. The kid was in a sacred place. The spirit was looking down on him. No way did he kill himself."

"What else, Ben?" Father John said. "Give me something else that'll make them change their minds."

"What's this to you?" Mistrust leaked into the Indian's voice.

Father John shook his head. "I don't like to see a man's death labeled suicide if it isn't true."

"I see." Ben leaned back against his chair, never taking his eyes away. "You're a real white do-gooder, aren't you, Father O'Malley? You're like the cavalry riding out against injustice wherever it raises its ugly head."

Father John swallowed back the phlegm of anger that rose in his throat. "Give me something to take to the white detective, Holden," he said. His voice was tight.

The Indian looked away a moment, considering. "I've been thinking," he said finally, a conciliatory tone now. "I think Duncan got himself into some serious trouble, and somebody followed him here from Denver. Waited until he went out to Bear Lake and killed him."

"You tell that to Detective Slinger?"

"Why don't you tell him? Maybe he'll listen to you."

Father John got to his feet, pulled open the door, and went outside. It was raining harder now, and he tipped his cowboy hat low over his forehead and started walking down the driveway. He didn't have much, but he had something: a guy who was looking for a job and planning to start work. Hardly somebody who was thinking about suicide. And there was more. Someone had followed Grover from Denver. It made sense. "The boss killed him," the man in the confessional had said.

He could imagine the conversation with Detective Slinger: *Who,* Father O'Malley? *Who* followed Grover? And he wouldn't be able to say . . .

Unless Grover had mentioned a name to Gus Iron Bear while he was taking instructions.

Father John decided to drive out to the medicine man's place before he went to see Slinger.

"You heard from her?" The voice sliced through the rain, and Father John looked around. Ben Holden stood in the middle of the driveway, about twenty feet away, slicker still unsnapped, black cowboy hat pushed back. Wetness glistened on his dark face.

"No," Father John said.

"Our boy Lucas is taking a job in Denver." Ben came a few steps closer. They might have been old friends, talking about a mutual acquaintance, somebody they both liked but hadn't seen for a while. "He'll keep an eye on her. She's been alone in the city, nobody around that cares about her. I've been worrying about her."

Father John nodded, then turned and continued down the driveway. "So have I," he said to himself.

# ❮ 5 ❯

The intercom buzzed twice. On the third buzz, Vicky
Holden forced her eyes away from the computer
screen, swiveled around, and pushed the button on
the small machine with the blinking red light.

"What is it?" She heard the irritation in her voice. She'd
left instructions with her secretary, Laola, to hold all calls.
There was an important meeting in a few minutes on the
appeal in the *Navajo Nation* v. *Lexcon Oil* case. The out-
come would determine who controlled the methane gas
on a lot of Indian land: the tribes or the corporations that
had managed to purchase the coal beds beneath the lands
years ago. It was the most important case she'd ever
worked on.

She'd come into it late, only a week after the federal
district court had ruled against the Navajo Nation. Wes
Nelson, the managing partner at Howard and Fergus, had
asked her to handle the appeal to the Tenth Circuit. She'd
jumped at the opportunity. Filed the notice of appeal and
designation of record, started writing the brief. And then,
the call from Jacob Hazen, the tribal lawyer. The Navajo
Nation might not want to go ahead with the appeal after
all.

Vicky had felt her heart sink. The federal district court

ruling affected all the tribes in the judicial district. It could impact the entire country. It could not stand! If the Navajos were getting nervous about moving ahead—the legal expenses, the uncertainty—well, she intended to present the strongest arguments possible to change their minds.

The meeting would start in ten minutes; the other lawyers were probably filing into the conference room now, and she still had some notes she wanted to finish.

"I'm very sorry, Vicky," Laola was saying, a new patina of city sophistication in her voice. The girl had been her secretary for almost two years, managing her one-attorney office in Lander with the precision of a drill sergeant. She insisted on coming to Denver when Vicky had decided to rejoin Howard and Fergus, where she'd worked after graduating from the University of Denver law school. Vicky had done her best to talk the young woman out of coming. Not even twenty-one—an Arapaho, like herself, used to the open spaces of the reservation. She could get lost in the city. There were times when Vicky felt lost herself. The girl had insisted.

In the end, Vicky had talked the firm into hiring her. Most of the time she was grateful for Laola's presence, grateful not to be the lone Indian riding the elevators to the thirty-seventh floor of the steel-and-glass tower that rose over Seventeenth Street. Still, Laola could be like a young filly pulling in her own direction.

"Who is it?" Vicky said.

"He won't give his name."

"What? Tell him to call back later."

"I tried that. He says I should tell you it's a matter of life and death."

Vicky threw her head back and stared at the ceiling. Her train of thought was derailed anyway. "Put him through," she said, but the phone was already buzzing.

She lifted the receiver. "Vicky Holden," she said, her tone now sharp with irritation.

"This is Vince Lewis." The voice boomed over the line, as if the man were shouting from the outer office. "I must speak with you."

"What is this about?" The name meant nothing to her.

"I have to see you today."

"Mr. Lewis," Vicky began, struggling to contain the growing sense of exasperation. "I have a full schedule. Perhaps my secretary can set up an appointment for next week." Next week, she was thinking, was already booked. She had to file the brief with the appellate court, unless the Navajos decided not to proceed. The possibility sent a little shiver through her.

"You're an Arapaho from Wind River Reservation, aren't you?"

Vicky took a moment. The conversation had lurched in an unexpected direction. Vince Lewis, whoever he was, had taken the trouble to find out about her. Whatever he wanted to talk about could affect her people.

"Hold on." She cradled the receiver into her shoulder, turned back to the computer, and tapped the keyboard. Today's schedule floated onto the screen. This morning's meeting—already starting—the brief to finish, two o'clock with a landlord about a lease, three o'clock with a couple in need of a new will. She was an expert on leases, wills, divorces, and custody matters, the everyday cases she'd handled the last five years in Lander and had hoped to escape in Denver. But every senior partner had an important client or friend who needed mundane legal help, and somehow the cases fell to her, inserting themselves around important matters like the Navajo Nation.

The couple could probably be rescheduled, she decided. Wills were seldom urgent.

She said, "I could see you at three." That would still give her an hour before she had to leave for DIA to pick up Lucas, who was flying in from Los Angeles at five. "You know where we're located?"

"You don't understand." The words were whipped with impatience. "Not your office. Not my office either. I'll meet you at the Ship's Tavern in the Brown Palace."

"Wait a minute—" Vicky began, then stopped. A vacancy, like the absence of sound in a vault, came over the line. She pushed the intercom button. "Laola, can you get the caller back?"

"I don't think so."

"Don't tell me that. Just do it."

"He wouldn't give his number."

Vicky drew in a long breath. "Reschedule my three o'clock," she said. Then she swiveled to the computer, clicked on print, and waited while the printer spewed out several pages. Jamming the pages into her leather folder, she headed out into the corridor, her heels sinking into the plush royal-blue carpet, past the cubicle where Laola worked, past a succession of doors with the partners' names discreetly emblazoned on bronze plaques, and past the doors to the associates' offices, one of which had been hers five years before.

Displayed on the walls between the offices were large oil paintings of mountains and lakes in gilded frames. Sometimes, in the corridors of Howard and Fergus, she felt as if she was drowning in the low hum of purposeful activity that emanated from behind the doors.

She rode the elevator to the top-floor conference room, wondering what she'd done. Canceled an appointment to meet someone she hadn't heard of fifteen minutes ago, and she had no idea what the meeting was about. No, that wasn't true. It was about the reservation.

The others—men in dark suits, ties knotted smartly at the collars of light-colored shirts—were already seated around the polished cherry conference table. On one side, Jacob Hazen was flanked by the two Navajo councilmen, their dark heads silhouetted against the windows that framed a view of the Rocky Mountains. Across from the Indians were three lawyers from Howard and Fergus, including Wes Nelson, the managing partner.

"There's been a new development," Wes explained as she slid into the vacant chair next to him.

As if on cue, Jacob Hazen leaned forward, bracing his stocky frame on both elbows. "Lexcon's proposed a settlement," he said.

"Settlement!" Vicky heard the astonishment in her voice. "The court ruled in their favor. Why would they want a settlement now? Everything's going their way."

One of the councilmen cleared his throat. "We hear a rumor Lexcon's found another methane gas field on the res. They're gonna want to give us a settlement in the old case, grease the wheels, you might say, so they can get on to drilling the new field. We're thinking we oughta consider an offer."

Vicky remained quiet. She was aware of the eyes on her. "What makes you think they've located another field?"

"They never quit looking." The Navajo gave a sharp laugh. "Flying planes over the res all the time, looking for methane coming up from the earth."

"They also collect data from satellites." Jacob Hazen nodded toward the windows and the endless sky with gray clouds breaking over patches of blue. "Commercial satellites up there, orbiting the earth, making images. Oil and gas companies buy data from satellite companies all the time."

"We're buying our own satellite data now." This from the other councilman. "No reason for Lexcon to know more than we know. We got a specialist to tell us what's going on." He pushed his chair back and began levering himself to his feet.

Vicky stayed seated. She heard her own voice going on about how the case was too important for the district court ruling to stand, about how the appellate brief was due next week, but the others were getting to their feet, chairs scudding backward on the carpet, papers crackling. A sense of futility as heavy as weights settled over her shoulders. How could she help them if they didn't want her help? Suddenly she felt glad she'd agreed to meet Vince Lewis this afternoon. If something had happened on the reservation, she wanted to know about it. Maybe she could help her own people.

Vicky stood up and turned to Wes. "Could I see you a moment?"

# ‹ 6 ›

"You may want to hold off on the brief," Wes said. His voice cut through the elevator's soundless, downward pressure.

Vicky was quiet. She had every intention of finishing the brief, even if she had to do it on her own time. She would call Hazen to reiterate the importance of going ahead with the appeal.

The elevator doors swooshed open, and they walked wordlessly down the corridor to a spacious office that was all royal-blue carpet, dark leather sofas and chairs, and glass-topped tables with silver vases and figurines that winked in the overhead light. Beyond the desk, a wall of windows framed a view of the dark clouds threading like smoke around the tops of adjacent skyscrapers.

Vicky took one of the leather chairs and waited until Wes had sat down in the high-backed chair behind the desk. Loosening the knot of his dark tie, unbuttoning the collar, rubbing his neck. "You've been doing a fine job on the Navajo case," he said. "No worries, I hope. No insecurities about being the only woman on the team."

"This isn't about the case, Wes."

The man's eyebrows shot up in a mixture of surprise and expectation. "No? What, then?"

"I got a call this morning from someone named Vince Lewis. What can you tell me about him?"

"Vince Lewis?" The lawyer let out a low whistle. "Very big man, Vicky. Vice-president of development at Baider Industries. What'd he want?"

"He wanted to see me this afternoon."

"No kidding!" A grin started at the corners of Wes's mouth and spread into a full smile. Light danced in his gray eyes. "You know what this means?"

"I hoped you could tell me."

"Baider Industries must be considering new counsel, and they're looking at Howard and Fergus." Wes threw a glance around the office as if to locate the place whence such good fortune had come. "Baider's been represented by Michaels, Starcroft and Loomis." He shrugged. "Nathan Baider and Loomis are friends from way back. But word on Seventeenth Street is that Nathan Jr.'s running the company now. Goes by the name of Roz, don't ask me why." Another shrug. "Could be Roz convinced the old man to hire new counsel."

So much had changed in the five years she'd been in Lander, Vicky was thinking. She was a half beat behind. She said, "I'm not familiar with Baider Industries."

"No? Well, let me fill you in." Wes laced his fingers together over the front of his shirt, the dark tie. "Big diamond mining company. Mines in Colorado, Wyoming, Canada. Mined some of the world's largest diamonds up there in Wyoming. The old man's a real immigrant success story. Fifteen years old when he got out of Germany two steps ahead of the Gestapo and landed in New York."

Wes leaned back in his chair, warming to the subject. "Worked his way west to Colorado and spent ten years mining molybdenum at Climax. Soaked up everything he could on geology and went looking for diamond deposits.

There's gold, silver, lead, molybdenum, tungsten, phosphate, and probably a thousand other minerals in the Rocky Mountains. But diamonds? Nobody'd heard much about diamonds until Nathan Baider got into the business. You ask me"—he leaned over the desk—"Nathan Baider still calls the shots. He's not the kind to let go. The company's his baby."

Vicky stood up and walked over to the large oil painting above the sofa: buffalo foraging in a snow-shrouded pasture. She turned back to the man at the desk. "If Baider Industries wants new counsel," she said, "why didn't the vice-president call you or one of the other senior partners? I'm the low person on the totem pole here."

Wes flashed her a tolerant smile. "Don't underestimate yourself. No doubt they've heard about you heading up the appeal on the Navajo case. Lawyers talk, you know." He gave her a conspiratorial smile.

Vicky walked back to her chair, then to the painting again. She could always think better when she was moving, a gift from the old ones, she supposed. Crossing the plains, always moving through the vast spaces. They had to think while they were moving. She said, "I think Lewis wants to tell me something about the reservation."

"Sit down, Vicky," Wes said. "You're making me nervous. Baider's in the diamond business. They operate mines in southern Wyoming. You ever heard of diamond deposits on the res?"

Vicky dropped into her chair. "No," she said simply. Oil, gas, gold, uranium, timber, water—the reservation was rich in natural resources. She'd never heard of diamonds.

"Let's imagine the conversation over at Baider Industries," Wes went on. "Roz decides it's time for new counsel, somebody up to date on natural resource laws and regulations. Any suggestions? Vince Lewis—his job is to keep track of such matters—says, 'Sharp female lawyer over at Howard and Fergus handling *Navajo v. Lexcon. Arapaho.* Natural interest in natural resources.' " He paused, grinning at her. "Roz says, 'Go have a talk with that phenomenal lady.' "

"At the Ship's Tavern?"

"Vicky, Vicky." The lawyer was shaking his head. "You've forgotten the street is a small village. Town criers always looking for news. So Vince meets you on neutral territory. Anybody who recognizes the two of you won't know what to think." Wes shrugged. "He's your classic movie-star type—tall, dark-haired, good-looking. Has a roving eye that his wife ignores. The two of you are having a friendly drink, that's all. But if you're spotted at the Baider building, or somebody sees Lewis here, Michaels, Starcroft and Loomis'll have the news in ten minutes. I suspect Roz'd like to line up new counsel before he cuts any ties."

"I don't know, Wes . . ."

"Trust me on this." The man pushed his chair back and got to his feet. "The meeting is a preliminary interview. Lewis'll ask some discreet questions, gauge your response, and try to figure out if you'd like to represent Baider Industries. You've got a mighty big fish on the line, Vicky. Reel it in, and we'll see that you're amply compensated."

Vicky hesitated. The uneasy sense that had gripped her during the brief conversation with Vince Lewis was still there. "He said it was a matter of life and death," she told the man standing on the other side of the desk.

"Hey, Nathan Baider built the company with that attitude. Everything's a matter of life and death at Baider Industries." He came around the desk, and Vicky got to her feet and followed him across the office. He flung open the door and stood back, waiting: the friendly, relaxed smile, the little wink. She stepped out into the corridor. "Let me know how the meeting goes," he called.

She kept going in the direction of her own office, the closed doors and oil paintings blurring past like moving trains. She'd forgotten how the game was played—Wes was right about that. But he was dead wrong about Vince Lewis. She would meet the man at the Ship's Tavern and she'd find out what was going on at the reservation that was a matter of life and death.

# ‹ 7 ›

It was almost three when Vicky struck out for the Brown Palace Hotel a block away, joining the knots of people scurrying along Seventeenth Street, umbrellas floating overhead. Skyscrapers rose around her, like the cliffs of a concrete canyon, the spires lost in the dense gray clouds. Rain spattered the pavement and pinged against the cars that crawled past, windshield wipers swinging in crazy rhythms. The air smelled of gasoline and stale food, so unlike the smells of sage and wild grasses that came with the rain on the reservation.

At the Tremont Place intersection, she waited for the light to change. The traffic spewed flumes of dirt-gray water into the air. Across the street, the doorman at the Brown Palace stood under the striped awning and blew on a whistle, beckoning a cab half a block away. The whistling noise was muffled in the sounds of the traffic splashing past.

On the diagonal corner, several men in dark raincoats stepped off the curb and started across Seventeenth Street, collars pulled up around their heads. Only one carried an umbrella. Vince Lewis. Tall, dark-haired, good-looking guy—movie-star type. Wes had gotten the description right.

The others made a precision turn to the right and headed down the side of the hotel, but Lewis kept walking toward the entrance, shoulders held back, dark, curly head held high.

The light turned green. As Vicky stepped off the curb in unison with the little crowd around her, she saw the black sedan bearing down Tremont Place. Instinctively she jumped back, stomach muscles clinched, fingers tightened around the strap of her black bag. She felt someone take hold of her arm and yank her out of the way as the sedan made a wide arc through the street, then bumped over the opposite curb and onto the sidewalk. She stood frozen in place. It was heading straight at Lewis. The man pedaled backward, holding out the umbrella, as if it might stop the oncoming destruction.

There was a thud of compacted weight against bones and flesh. The man was thrown upward, suspended above the hood a half second before he crashed into the windshield and crumbled onto the sidewalk. The sedan bounced over the curb and sped through the red light. Traffic squealed to a stop, tires sliding on the wet asphalt.

Vicky caught the last three numbers on the plate— 672—and the make: a Camry.

She broke through the other pedestrians and ran to the man on the sidewalk. One leg bent sideways over the umbrella, arms flung out, dark hair wet and matted about his head. Blood spurted through a gash that ran from his temple along his cheek and laid open the pink raw flesh inside. There was a stillness, an air of resignation about him, as if he knew that the most vital part of him was preparing to leave and there was nothing he could do.

She dropped to her knees and curled her hand over the crown of his head to keep the spirit from departing, the way she remembered the medicine man treating her grandfather when she was a child.

"Send an ambulance!" someone shouted into a cell phone.

"Let me through. I'm a doctor." A man's voice came from behind. Vicky felt someone shove against her. Reluctantly she removed her hand and got to her feet. "Please don't leave," she said out loud so that the spirit would hear.

A large man brushed past and dropped to one knee. He began probing the unconscious man's wrist, then the carotid artery. Seconds passed. Finally he removed his own raincoat and laid it over the prone man. A siren sounded in the distance.

Vicky stepped back through the crowd flowing around her like water, until she could no longer see the body sprawled on the pavement. A mixture of dread and nausea welled inside her. Stuck in her mind, like a still from a movie, was the image of the movie-star-handsome man in the black raincoat suspended over the hood of the sedan.

The siren grew louder, piercing the sounds of the rain on the sidewalk. A red-and-white ambulance drew alongside the curb ahead of the black squad car pulling in. Two officers in dark blue uniforms emerged from the car and shouldered their way through the crowd, shouting orders to stand back. Slowly a path opened, and the ambulance attendants hurried across the sidewalk.

"Anybody see what happened?" one of the officers shouted.

Several people raised their hands.

The officer produced a small pad from inside his jacket and began moving around the periphery of the crowd, asking questions, jotting notes in the rain.

"I saw it happen," Vicky said when he approached.

"Your name?" His tone was calm, matter-of-fact, the narrow, reddish face unreadable.

She gave him her name, address, telephone numbers, and told him about the black Camry speeding up, jumping the curb, running down the man. The words spilling out, as if the horrible image in her mind might be washed away by the torrent. She drew in a breath and told him the last three license-plate numbers.

"It was deliberate," she said, watching the stretcher being wheeled across the sidewalk toward the ambulance. "The driver wanted to kill him."

"We'll need a complete statement from you tomorrow." His eyes held hers a moment before he turned toward another woman who had raised her hand.

"Officer," Vicky said. He glanced back. "I was on my way to meet someone named Vince Lewis. It may have been him."

"Wait here." He began shouldering his way through the cluster of silent people toward his partner. After a moment, he was back. "Driver's license says Vincent R. Lewis. You know him?"

"He was a potential client. It was an initial meeting." She heard herself parroting what Wes Nelson had said earlier, struggling to make it sound convincing. "Where are they taking him?"

"Denver Health." The officer was writing again, flipping over a page, starting another. "Like I said." He raised his eyes to hers, "We're gonna want a complete statement tomorrow."

Vicky nodded and turned toward the entrance of the Brown Palace. The ambulance was sliding away from the curb, its siren bouncing off the hotel's brown stone walls.

"Taxi, please," Vicky told the doorman standing limp-armed under the awning, eyes on the ambulance receding down the street.

He seemed to snap to attention. Stepping off the curb, he jammed the whistle between his lips and sent out a long, shrill noise that blended into the wail of the siren.

Vicky held the lapels of her raincoat closed against the chill passing through her and waited until a Yellow Cab pulled into the curb. Then she tipped the doorman and got into the rear seat. "Denver Health," she said.

Ten minutes later she was hurrying along the covered walkway that connected the redbrick hospital buildings on the outskirts of downtown Denver. The rain beat on the roof, and the cold wind swirled through the walkway, bending the stalks of tulips that poked out of the pots on both sides. Inside the glass entrance, a middle-aged black woman was leafing through a stack of papers at the information desk. Vicky asked for the emergency room, and the woman nodded toward the escalator in the building's atrium.

Vicky gripped the arm hold as the escalator rose to the second-story balcony. Nurses and doctors in green scrubs hurried past the groups of people standing along the railing, staring down into the atrium, dejection and hope etched in their expressions. She followed the signs down a corridor to another desk, where another middle-aged receptionist sat hunched over an opened newspaper. Beyond the desk was a double-steel door with an intercom panel on the adjacent wall.

"Excuse me," Vicky said.

The woman barely lifted her eyes. Vicky could see traces of pink scalp beneath the gray curls.

"Has Vince Lewis been brought in?"

"One moment," the woman said, pulling a clipboard out from the newspaper and running a finger down a column of names. "Vincent R. Lewis," she said without looking up. "He was just brought in."

"How is he?"

"You family?" Eyes still on the clipboard, as if the response was bound to be positive, but the question had to be asked. Regulations had to be followed.

"No."

The gray head snapped back, and the woman peered up at her. "I can only give information to a family member."

"You don't understand. I saw what happened."

The woman seemed to study her a moment, making up her mind. Finally she reached across the opened newspaper and picked up a phone. "Your name?"

Vicky gave her name.

"You can wait over there." She nodded toward an area across the hall from the steel doors while simultaneously pressing some keys on the phone.

Vicky walked over to the waiting area, the woman's voice trailing behind: "Someone named Vicky Holden's here about the hit-and-run victim. Says she saw the accident."

There was a stale odor of hopelessness in the waiting room that permeated the gray carpet, the worn chairs, the tables with thumbed-through magazines scattered across the top. A pop machine and ice maker hummed in the far corner. Vicky sank into the chair inside the entrance, ignoring the young couple seated side by side across the room, the look of relief and expectancy in their faces, as if news of another tragedy might lighten the burden of their own. She didn't want to trade stories. She wanted to think. On the other side of the steel doors, a man who had been on his way to see *her* could be dying.

And it was no coincidence. She knew it with the cold certainty that gripped her when a witness was lying on the stand. She had never tried to explain the knowing, never tried to fix a name—sixth sense, intuition—the way white people did. She accepted that she knew.

"I demand to see Vince Lewis." The sound of a man's voice, angry and insistent, came from around the corner. Vicky stood up and walked back into the corridor. A short, broad-backed man in a gray suit, gray raincoat bundled under one arm, pounded a fist on the desk.

"I'm sorry, sir, but if you're not family—" The receptionist was gripping the newspaper. She looked as if she might burst into tears.

"I'm his employer. Tell your superior I have the right to see him."

"Are you Nathan Baider?" Vicky walked over.

The man whirled about, the blue eyes sizing her up, she felt, then dismissing her: Indian woman. He looked younger than she'd thought at first, despite the red puffiness in his cheeks and the two vertical creases between his eyes. "Do I know you?" he barked.

"Vicky Holden. I had an appointment with Mr. Lewis this afternoon."

The man continued staring. "Yes, I'm Nathan Baider," he said finally. "You saw Vince this afternoon?"

Vicky shook her head. "I was on my way to meet him when he was hit."

"You a friend of his?" Still trying to place her, Vicky thought.

She began explaining: she was an attorney at Howard and Fergus; Lewis had called—

He held up a fleshy hand. "We have a law firm that handles company legal business." As he started to turn back to the desk, something behind her caught his attention.

"Jana," he called, stepping past her.

Vicky glanced around. A woman with stylishly cut auburn hair pushed behind her ears and a determined control in the perfectly made-up face was coming down the corridor, her long black raincoat hanging open over a black dress.

"Dastardly thing to happen," Baider said, taking her hand. "Don't worry. I'll see that the doctors do everything possible."

"Where is he?" The woman withdrew her hand and walked over to the receptionist. "Where is my husband?" she said in a tone accustomed to being obeyed.

Baider was at her side again. "This is Lewis's wife," he said. "I demand that you take us in."

The gray-haired woman hesitated, then got to her feet, maintaining a space between herself and the stocky man as she came around the desk. She walked over to the steel doors and leaned into the intercom panel, throwing nervous glances over one shoulder. A buzzing noise sounded, and she pushed the doors open. Without waiting for the couple, who fell in behind, she headed down a corridor lit like an aquarium and lined with gurneys and steel poles that dangled plastic bottles. Slowly the steel doors closed.

Vicky checked her watch. Twenty to five. It would take forty minutes to get to DIA, longer in the rush hour. She'd never make it before Lucas's plane arrived. She found her cell phone in her bag and dialed information. In a few seconds she was connected to the airport, arranging to leave a message for her son, the old feeling of failure nudging its way into her consciousness. She could imagine the expectant look on Lucas's face when he arrived at the gate, the dark eyes darting about, the ready smile dissolving into disappointment and, finally, into acceptance.

There would be a page: "Lucas Holden. Please pick up

the white courtesy phone." And the message: *Sorry. See you at the house.*

Vicky walked back to the waiting area and sat down. The young couple stared into the center of the room with the absorbed resignation that, she knew, mirrored her own.

She would wait. She was the attorney Vincent R. Lewis had risked his life to talk to. She would not leave until someone came through the steel doors and told her whether or not he was alive.

"Vicky?"

She glanced around at the tall, sandy-haired man standing in the entrance. Steve Clark, an old friend from undergraduate days in Denver, now a police detective, dressed in tan slacks and navy-blue sport coat and white shirt, with the knot of his red tie slightly loosened at the collar. Still handsome, in a more mature way, still the confident smile and intense brown eyes.

"What are you doing here?" Walking around in front of her chair, he reached down and took her hand. The warmth of his palm against hers made her realize how chilled she was.

"I could ask you the same question." She withdrew her hand slowly.

"I'm working on a hit-and-run case."

"So am I."

She drew in a breath and heard herself giving the same explanation she'd given Nathan Baider ten minutes before. When she finished, Steve took her hand again. "I didn't know you were back. Why didn't you call me?"

She stared at him. Had he heard anything she'd said? It had been six years, a lifetime ago, since they'd meant anything to each other.

"I'm sorry," she said. In the look that he bestowed on

her, she saw that he understood that she was sorry things had not turned out the way he'd hoped all those years ago.

"Can we talk about Vince Lewis?" she hurried on. "Is he going to make it?"

Steve gave a little shrug. "Let's hope so," he said. "They just wheeled him into surgery. No sense in you hanging around. Could be several hours."

She repeated what she'd told the officer earlier, then found a business card in her bag, scribbled her home number on the back, and handed it to him. "Call me as soon as you know anything," she said.

# ‹ 8 ›

The cab crawled through the rain along Speer Boulevard, wipers slashing at the windshield, water from other cars running over the hood. The driver let Vicky out at the downtown garage where she kept the Bronco. Within ten minutes she was heading west on Speer again. Lights from the skyscrapers winked in the rearview mirror. Ahead, the mountains were lost in banks of descending gray clouds.

She crossed the viaduct into north Denver, swung onto Twenty-ninth Avenue, and continued west, finally stopping in front of the 1890s farmhouse she'd rented. The white stucco house occupied a little bluff surrounded by the Victorians and cubelike bungalows of later decades that lined both sides of the block. A remnant of another time, the farmhouse, like her people.

She ducked out into rain-blurred headlights from the taxi drawing in behind. Her pumps sank into the soggy grass while she waited for Lucas to pay the driver and emerge from the backseat. He was as tall and as handsome as his father. More so, she thought: the black hair glistening in the rain, the still-innocent look in the narrow, sculptured face. He shrugged into the straps of a bulky red backpack and came toward her.

"Hey, Mom," he said.

She threw her arms around him, pulled his head down to hers, and kissed him. His cheeks felt warm beneath the cool slick of rain. She could hardly believe he'd taken a job in Denver. For the first time in years she would be in the same town as one of her kids.

"Come inside. You're drenched." She took his hand and led him up the concrete steps to the porch, her other hand fumbling for the key in the bag dangling from her shoulder. She let him in first and reached around to flip on the light in the entry. "Let me put your jacket on the coattree," she said. "I can set your backpack in the living room."

"Mom, what's next?" He was smiling. "Some hot cocoa?"

"Would you like some?"

He threw back his head and laughed, a low, relaxed sound that rebounded off the stucco walls. Pinpricks of light danced in his dark eyes.

She followed him through the archway into the living room on the left and turned on a table lamp. The light lapped over the gray sofa and chair, the tiled coffee table, and the TV cabinet that she'd brought from Lander.

"Looks like home." Lucas stood in the center of the room, glancing about.

She felt a sharp stab of pain. By the time she'd moved back to Lander, after undergrad and law school and three years at Howard and Fergus, Lucas and Susan were grown, on their own in Los Angeles. They'd never lived in the rented bungalow in Lander. In her mind, their childhood was forever compressed into the image of two small faces distorted behind the screen door of her mother's house as she'd driven away fifteen years ago, telling herself that she'd be back, and knowing, just as Susan and Lucas had known, that it wasn't true.

The memory always left her weak-kneed. Lucas was twenty-four years old now. She'd been nineteen when he was born. He was at least six feet tall, at least six inches taller than she was, with a lanky, muscular build, the dark complexion and neatly trimmed black hair, still shiny wet, and the handsome face with the little crook in the long nose—the mark of her people.

"You look like your father," she blurted.

He gave a nonchalant shrug, walked over to the window, and pushed back the edge of the lace curtain. Lights from the passing cars elongated into red-and-white smears across the glass.

"Sorry about the airport," she said. She was thinking: the lost years.

"No problem, Mom." He threw a little smile over one shoulder, then turned back to the window. "Something must've come up."

Vicky sat down in the middle of the sofa. She stopped herself from blurting out that Ben's drinking and beatings had come up. She said, "A man I was supposed to meet was hit by a car this afternoon."

"Jeez, Mom. I'm sorry," Lucas said. Then, a hint of impatience in his tone: "How do you get involved in this stuff, Mom?"

"What?"

"Dad worries about you, you know. Susan and I worry, too. You're always putting yourself in danger. We thought you'd change after you had to shoot that guy."

Vicky drew in her breath at the sting of the reminder. Less than six months before—a world ago—she had shot a man. Justifiable homicide in defense of another was the official ruling, but the legal explanations, the justifications, could never diminish the horror of it. It was one of the reasons she had left Lander.

"The man this afternoon was a potential client." She stopped herself from saying that Vince Lewis had wanted to tell her something about the reservation. "It was a hit-and-run," she went on. "I saw it happen."

Lucas crossed the room and sat down beside her, his eyes clouded in concern. He put a hand on her arm and squeezed it lightly. "Promise me you won't get involved."

"I'm a witness, Lucas. The police expect me to give a formal statement tomorrow."

"So tell them what you saw and let them find the driver. Promise you'll leave it at that, Mom."

Vicky set her hand over his. "I promise that I won't be in any danger." She hurried on, before he could object: "Tell me about your new job."

He shrugged and gave her the same mischievous grin he used to give her when he was a kid. "Information specialist, keep all the systems up and running. How much do you really want to know?" He took his hand from hers and waved away the question. "I've been thinking about leaving L.A. for some time. Now that you're here, well, Denver looked pretty good. I can look after you. Dad thinks it's a great idea." He seemed to be studying her for a reaction. "Dad's not drinking anymore," he said.

Vicky nodded. She'd gotten the news on the moccasin telegraph: Ben out of rehab, back at his old job as foreman on the Arapaho Ranch. She smiled at the irony. Ben always landed on his feet, while the ground beneath her was always slipping away.

She tried to focus on what Lucas was saying, something about an Arapaho from Oklahoma jumping off a cliff, about Ben making the arrangements to send the body back to Oklahoma for burial.

"Dad says everybody on the res is pretty upset the sheriff called it suicide. The sheriff jumped to conclusions, Dad says, so they could close the case. The guy was on a vision quest at Bear Lake."

"Bear Lake!" It was preposterous. The spirits were in the cliffs at Bear Lake, their images carved into the sandstone. It was a sacred place. A man on a vision quest would have been waiting for the spirits to speak to him. He wouldn't kill himself! He wouldn't defile a holy place like Bear Lake.

Vicky stood up, walked over to the window, and pushed back the lace curtain, the way Lucas had done. Rain washed down the other side of the black glass. A wavy stream of headlights moved along the street below. Ben was probably right. The sheriff was eager to close the case. White authorities didn't want to hear about holy places and vision quests. Again she felt an old sense of failure moving over her skin like a fever. She should be with her people. She could talk to the sheriff, explain the Arapaho Way.

"You okay, Mom?" Lucas's voice broke through her thoughts.

"Come on," she said, walking back to him. "I'll show you to your room." She waited while he grabbed his backpack, then led him through the dining room, up the narrow steps, and into the rear sleeping porch with a twin bed and the dresser she'd cleaned out for him. The warm air from the floor vents rustled the white curtains she'd had cleaned and rehung on the windows.

A few moments later, when Lucas had returned to the living room, she said, "What sounds good for dinner? Mexican; Italian?"

"Flat bread," he said, "and Indian stew and maybe a buffalo burger."

She was about to tell him that she knew just the restaurant when the phone rang. She hurried through the shadows of the dining room to the phone on the small table beneath the window. Even before she picked up the receiver, before she heard the familiar voice—"Vicky?"— she felt her muscles tense.

"Vince Lewis is dead," Steve told her.

The truth hit her like a clap of thunder. Vince Lewis had worked for a diamond mining company. There were no diamond deposits on Arapaho lands, as far as she knew, but he'd had information about the reservation, she was certain. *A matter of life and death,* he'd said. *His* death. Somebody had killed him to prevent him from talking to her, and she was going to have to find out why.

# ❮ 9 ❯

I t was almost noon before Father John got away from the ringing phones, the parishioners stopping by to visit, the correspondence he'd been trying to catch up on, and started for Gus Iron Bear's place. He'd been driving for most of an hour—*Tosca* playing beside him—when he turned north on Maverick Springs Road. North again through the open spaces cut with arroyos and filled with scrub brush and wild grasses. Crowheart Butte lifted into the sky ahead. The butte was sacred, a place of the spirits. This was an area of sacred places.

Another ten miles and he saw the clump of buildings on a rise ahead: white house, storage shed, pitched-roof barn. He took a right, bouncing across the rutted, muddy yard, and stopped in front of the house a couple of feet from the stoop. Slowly he unfolded his long legs and let himself out. He stood by the pickup, waiting. If Gus was ready to see him, someone would come out.

The door opened. Theresa Iron Bear, a small woman with white hair in thick braids that hung down the front of a red blouse, stood in the opening. "Come on in, Father," she called.

"How are you, Grandmother?" he said, using the polite term. Removing his cowboy hat, he stepped into the rectangular living room. A table lamp cast a dim circle of light over the upholstered chairs, sofa, and television arranged around the Indian rug in the center of the linoleum floor. The odor of burned sage permeated the air.

"Have a seat, Father." The old woman gestured toward the sofa. Then, disappearing down a hallway that led to the bedrooms, she called out, "I'll get Gus."

Father John sat down and waited, turning his hat between his knees a few minutes before tossing it on the cushion beside him. Beyond the window on the other side of the room, the plains, tinged with green, rolled like waves into the sky. The clouds had turned black, filled with rain.

A couple of minutes passed before the stooped figure of the medicine man emerged from the hallway. He looked older than Father John remembered—drawn and frail, dark eyes sunken beneath the curve of his brow. Father John got to his feet. "It's good to see you, Grandfather."

He waited until Gus had settled into the worn-looking chair by the lamp before resuming his own seat. For one crazy moment—the way the light washed over the old man's forehead and cheekbones—Gus resembled a spirit. An untrue person, the Arapahos would say.

After the usual exchange of pleasantries—the rain, the crafts fair; it was never polite to come to the point right away—Gus said, "You come about Duncan, didn't you?"

Father John shifted forward on the sofa and clasped his hands between his knees. "What can you tell me about him, Grandfather?"

The old man cleared his throat and rearranged his slight frame in the chair. "The kid drove into the yard. Stumbled out of the truck, crying like a woman. I says to myself, he's drunk, but he was sober as the day the Creator give him breath. He was like a wild horse that finally give up and let himself be led into the corral. A wild one that got sick of his wildness."

Gus took a gulp of air, his eyes turned away, remembering. "Kid says to me, 'Help me, Grandfather.' Says, 'I wanna get off the white road and on the Indian road.' Says, 'I need the spiritual power to keep on livin'.' My heart went out to him. I said, you take instructions, learn the right ways, then you can go on a vision quest to the rock carvings where the spirits are. I told him the spirits would give him the power he needed. So he started taking instructions. Moved out here and bunked in the barn."

"When was that, Grandfather?" It had started to rain. Drops of water speckled the windowpane.

"Three weeks to the day before he was killed." The old man's lips worked around the words. "It wasn't long enough, but he was in a big hurry to go on the quest. Summer isn't come yet, I told him. That's the best time for a vision quest. But he'd been with white folks that want everything right now. Don't have patience to wait for the right time. He had soul sickness."

The quiet lengthened between them, like the gray daylight creeping through the window and mingling with the lamplight. After a long moment Gus started talking again. "Go to Bear Lake, I told him. Take your pipe and some sage. Cleanse yourself in the lake and climb up the path to the ledge below the spirit rock. You won't have nothing to eat, nothing to drink. Just smoke the pipe and pray to the spirit in the rock. You must make yourself ready, I say, in case the spirits decide to come and give you power."

Gus lifted his head and stared at the ceiling. The rain beat hard on the roof. "After he went to Bear Lake, I heard the first thunder, before the rains started. Means a long life, when you hear the first thunder. I figured it was a good sign. Duncan would've heard it, too. But the thunder got louder, crashing around the sky, real angry. I knew the spirits was angry 'cause the boy wasn't ready yet. I let him go too soon. I knew they was gonna test him. He was supposed to be patient. Be accepting. Keep praying. But he wasn't strong enough. He got scared and tried to get away."

Suddenly the old man dropped his head into his hands and began sobbing quietly. The thin shoulders twitched against the back of the chair. After a moment he looked up. "The spirits could've come like eagles, swooping down on him, or badgers or deer running after him, or rattlers. They was testing him." His voice was so soft, Father John could barely hear the words. "Or maybe the thunder keeper came. Thunder is strong when it gets angry. It can kill."

Father John looked away. This was not the information he'd hoped for. He could imagine the white detective's expression when Gus explained that Duncan Grover couldn't have committed suicide. He was killed by the spirits. Ironically both the medicine man and the detective had come to the same conclusion: the kid had hurled himself off the cliff.

The old man was watching him, waiting for his reaction. "Grandfather," he began, taking a different tack, "Ben thinks Duncan was running from something. Did he mention any trouble in Denver? Say that somebody was following him?"

The old man blinked into the lamplight and shook his head. "Maybe Duncan was the one following somebody."

Father John could hear the sound of his own breathing. It would explain why Grover had run to the reservation, instead of to Oklahoma, where he had family. *He* was following somebody.

"What makes you think so, Grandfather?" he said.

"Three days ago the phone rang." The old man shifted his gaze sideways to the phone on top of the TV stand. "A girl. Says she has to talk to Duncan. I told her Duncan wasn't back from Bear Lake." The old man's eyes clouded over. "Didn't know he wasn't ever coming back," he said. Then, his voice stronger: "The girl says have him call me at the convenience store."

*Convenience store.* There must be a half-dozen convenience stores in the area. He could visit them all, but who would he ask for? A girl who had wanted to talk to a murdered man? She didn't come forward when Duncan's body was found, or Banner would have mentioned her. Whoever she was, Father John decided, she didn't want to get involved.

He said, "Duncan ever mention her?"

"Not in words." Gus shook his head. "But I been doin' some thinking. I think that's why he wanted to get on the straight road, 'cause there was a woman that didn't want him otherwise." The old man held his gaze a long moment. "Duncan said he'd been stayin' in Lander before he moved his bedroll into the barn. I been thinking. Maybe he was staying with her."

"Did you tell this to Detective Slinger?" Father John suspected the answer.

"Told the detective about the spirits and Duncan's vision quest. He didn't wanna hear any of it." A kind of hopelessness came into the old man's eyes. "I'm afraid it's my fault the boy's dead."

Father John got to his feet and set his arm on the old man's shoulder. "Listen to me, Grandfather. It is not your fault."

Gus tilted his head back and looked at him with a mixture of grief and trust. He nodded.

Father John thanked the old man and let himself out. He checked his Timex. One-thirty. Another hour and he could be at Bear Lake. Before he paid a visit to Detective Slinger, he wanted to see the sacred place where Duncan Grover had been murdered.

# ◀ 10 ▶

Leaving the Wind River Reservation.

Father John passed the sign and continued north on Highway 287 through a landscape of flat-topped buttes that glowed pink in the aftermath of the rain. The sounds of *Faust*—"De l'enfer qui vient"—mingled with the hum of the Toyota's engine, the thump of the tires. He crossed Bear Creek, Indian Meadows passing outside the window. A few more miles, and he turned west off the highway and started up a narrow road into the foothills, the Toyota straining against the climb. Black clouds still formed over the mountains, threatening more rain.

More rain. That meant a day or two before he could call another practice for the St. Francis Eagles, the baseball team he'd started seven years ago, that first summer at the mission, when he'd needed a baseball team to coach. Only three practices so far this season. The kids were looking good: Chester Wallowing Bull sprinting for a grounder, sliding through the mud, coming up grinning, the ball gloved. Joseph Antelope covering first like a pro. The kid's dad, Eldon, had played first base in the minors twenty years ago, and he'd agreed to help coach this season.

Father John felt the old excitement at the prospect of

the new season, and yet—Duncan Grover was still on his mind. Alone in the mountains, on a cliff, hungry, thirsty. Lightning flashing, thunder erupting. Thunder kills. But it wasn't thunder that had killed Grover. It was the boss. *There's gonna be more murders.* The words cut through his thoughts like a harsh, dissonant melody.

Ahead, the road emptied into a high mountain valley, ringed with slopes of pines, topped by red sandstone cliffs—the place of the spirits. Bear Lake lay ahead, placid and self-contained in the gray afternoon light. He came around a bend and pulled off into a clearing near a clump of willows. In the distance was the sound of thunder, as crisp as a drumbeat.

It might have been here, he thought, getting out of the pickup, that Duncan Grover had waded into the lake, hands grasping at the willows for support, feet sinking into the sandy bottom. He had cleansed himself in preparation to meet the spirits.

Father John tilted his head back and scanned the red sandstone cliffs above. The spirits don't show themselves to everybody, the elders had told him. Only to those who are worthy.

It was a couple of minutes before he saw the petroglyph: a large, white humanlike figure carved onto the flat face of a red sandstone cliff. The guardian—the keeper—of the valley. In the Old Time, an elder had once explained, the spirit had kept the deer and sheep in the valley so the people could find food. Now the spirit protected the valley from harm.

Father John walked along the shore looking for the path up the mountain to the petroglyph. He'd gone about fifty yards when he spotted the depression in the ground, a mud-filled gully that meandered upward through the pines. The thunder crashed again, shaking the ground.

There was a flash of lightning above the cliffs.

He started uphill, walking fast. He didn't want to be on the mountain during a storm. The path lay in shadow, disappearing at times, then reappearing. Pine branches grabbed at his jacket and scratched at his hands and face.

He'd gained about three hundred feet in elevation, he guessed, when he stopped. His boots were caked with mud. He gulped at the thin air, his heart pounding against his ribs. Bear Lake floated in the shadows below, and on the cliffs across the valley, he could see other white figures emerging out of the red sandstone. Symbols of other spirit guardians: the deer, keeper of the animals; the eagle, keeper of the wingeds; the thunder, keeper of the atmosphere. In the winter, the elder had said, you could hear the spirits chipping out their own reflections in the cliffs.

He resumed the climb, pacing himself now. The path was steep, and he had to dig his boots into the soft earth to keep from sliding backward. His calf muscles protested, and his breath came in ragged, painful spasms that punctuated the sound of the wind in the pines. At an outcropping of boulders, he stopped again and looked up.

He could see the petroglyph clearly: squared body, arms extended in a kind of blessing. There were three fingers on each hand, three toes on each foot. An elaborate headdress fanned around the squared head. Large, round eyes looked out from the masked face. Below the petroglyph was a rock ledge that jutted from the cliff like the proscenium of a stage.

He took in another gulp of air and started climbing up the boulder field, pulling himself hand over hand, jamming his boots into the cracks between the large rocks to keep from falling backward. Finally he hoisted himself onto the ledge. He'd been climbing for over an hour.

The valley spread below, nearly lost in the blue-black

shadows creeping down the mountainsides. A sense of peace came over him, the peace Duncan Grover must have felt, he thought, as he'd lifted his pipe to the four directions and asked the spirits for the power to change his life. The same prayer he himself had made during his own retreat in Boston two years ago, he realized.

He moved along the edge, his eyes sweeping over the drop-off, searching for the place where Duncan had fallen. On the far side of the ledge, the boulder field sloped onto the top of a perpendicular rock wall that dropped a couple hundred feet into the trees. Detective Slinger was right. If Grover had accidentally stepped off the ledge, the boulder field would have stopped his fall. He would have had to take a running jump to fly out over the field and fall down the wall.

*The boss killed him.* Father John crouched down, keeping his gaze on the wall, trying to picture exactly how it had happened. Grover, praying, smoking his pipe. Semiconscious, perhaps, waiting for the spirits to come in a vision.

Instead, two men climb onto the ledge. The boss approaches, strikes him with a pipe. Then drags his body to the far end and hurls him over the ledge. A strong man, the boss. Ben Holden said that Grover looked in good shape.

As he stood up, Father John saw a flash of motion, like that of a deer or coyote darting through the trees on the far side of the valley. He kept his eyes on the spot. There was a clap of thunder, another bolt of lightning, and he saw the figure of a man running across an opening, then he was gone. Father John had the odd sense that the person he'd seen across the valley had also seen him.

He climbed off the ledge and started down through the boulder field, leaning into the rocks, grabbing the sharp edges for support. The air was hazy with rain. Thunder rolled across the peaks, like a giant coughing himself awake.

He reached the base of the field and started walking down the path, the thunder following, crashing behind him. Lightning split the sky, and the first drops of rain stung his face and hands. Another possibility worked its way into his consciousness: maybe somebody didn't want Duncan Grover in this place, on the ledge, close to the petroglyph. And maybe the man across the valley just now hadn't wanted him in this place either.

He rejected the idea almost as it formed. People came to the valley all the time. They drove up the road, stopped at the lake, stared up at the cliffs hoping for a glimpse of the spirits. Why would anyone kill Duncan Grover for coming here?

By the time he reached the Toyota, the rain was hard and cold, the thunder more insistent. A streak of lightning was so bright that for a second it seemed as if the sun had suddenly broken through. His jacket was soaked; even his shirt clung to his skin.

He drove back down the mountains, threading his way through streams washing over the road. He knew what had happened to Grover: it was as clear as a vision. But some of what he knew he couldn't talk about. He was going to have to find another way to convince a white detective in Lander that Grover hadn't killed himself. Somebody had hurled him off the ledge.

It was dark when Father John turned into the mission. The rain had stopped a few miles north of Riverton, but gray fog had pressed down on the highway, swallowing up the remaining daylight. The street lamps around Circle

Drive sent wan circles of light over the grounds. He parked next to the dark sedan in front of the administration building. A parishioner to see Father Ryan, he thought.

As he started up the front steps, a dark-haired woman in a red raincoat burst through the door, weaving against the railing, nearly stumbling on the steps. He reached out to steady her, but she ducked past and kept going.

"Wait a minute," he called, starting after her. She was already at the sedan, flinging open the door, folding herself inside.

He caught the door and held it open against her efforts to yank it shut. "Let me go!" she screamed up at him. Tears ran down her cheeks; green and black smudges rimmed her eyes. She was probably about thirty, and beautiful, he thought, despite the anguish in her face.

"Can I help you?" He made his voice calm.

She was still looking at him, blinking with comprehension. Her nostrils flared in anger. "You're Father O'Malley," she said.

"Yes. What's going on?"

"You'll find out soon enough." She pulled at the door, but he held on to it. "Let me go."

"Tell me what happened. Who are you?"

She kept her hand on the handle. "Mary Ann Williams. Remember the name, Father O'Malley, because you're going to hear it again. You and Father Ryan are going to pay for what you've done."

"What's this all about?" he said, but he was talking to himself. The door shut, the engine turned over, and the sedan lurched backward, then forward onto Circle Drive. Gravel sprayed his hands and face. The car sped toward Seventeen Mile Road, flashing past the grove of cottonwoods, and then it was gone.

He whirled around and went inside to find Don Ryan.

# ‹ 11 ›

Father John strode down the corridor lined with portraits of the early Jesuits of St. Francis Mission, faces set in certitude, eyes solemn behind rimless glasses. The far door was open. His assistant stood at the window, looking out into the dim light, one hand braced against the frame.

"What's going on?" Father John stopped in the doorway.

The other priest remained motionless: there was only the smallest twitch of a muscle beneath his blue polo shirt. Finally he walked over to the desk. He kept his eyes straight ahead. "Just finished a counseling session," he said, sitting down, methodically rearranging a stack of file folders.

"The woman was crying. What happened?"

The other priest brushed some nonexistent dust from the top folder, then looked up. "She's going through a divorce, has a lot of issues. I've been trying to help her."

"Who is she?" Father John had never seen the woman before. She wasn't one of the whites from Riverton or Lander who occasionally came to Sunday Mass at the Indian church.

"Mary Ann Williams." The other priest's voice was flat.

He might have been describing the rain. "Lives over in Riverton."

"How long have you been counseling her?"

"What is this? The Inquisition? What difference does it make?" Father Don jumped up and walked back to the window. His breath made a little gray smudge on the glass. "Sorry," he said after a couple seconds. "I guess the session upset me, too."

"She said we're going to pay for what we've done to her," Father John persisted. "What's she talking about?"

"She said that?" The other priest swung around, a look of alarm in the pale eyes. Then, as if he had willed it so, the alarm dissolved into mild concern. "She has a depressive personality." His voice was steady. "She'll probably feel better tomorrow."

"Somebody should check on her now," Father John said. "Does she have family, friends in town?"

"How would I know?" The alarm returned.

Father John walked over and picked up the phone. "The Riverton police will send someone out on a welfare check."

"The police!" Father Don was across the office, his arm flashing out, yanking the phone away. "You want a squad car to pull up in front of her apartment building? You want to send her over the edge?"

"She shouldn't be alone," Father John said. "Where does she live? I can go over."

The other priest stared at him a moment. Then he went over to the coattree and grabbed a jacket. "Mary Ann doesn't know you," he said. "I'll check on her myself." He walked out the door. The sound of his footsteps receded down the corridor, and then the front door slammed shut, sending a ripple of motion through the old walls.

•  •  •

By the time Father John had locked up the administration building and walked over to the residence, darkness had descended through the fog. There was no sign of Father Don's blue sedan.

The residence groaned like an old rocking chair as he let himself in the front door. Walks-On stood at the end of the hall, tail wagging into the kitchen. Elena had already gone home, but there would be a note on the kitchen table. *Stew in oven, turn on coffee.* He could recite the instructions by heart.

He went into the kitchen, shook some dried food into the dog's dish, then dished up his own plate of stew and sat down at the table, his thoughts jumping between Duncan Grover and the woman running out of Father Don's office.

After dinner, he put a tape of *Faust* into the player on the bookcase in his study and spent the evening at his desk working on the summer schedule: marriage preparation classes, religious-ed classes, Arapaho culture programs, new parent groups. And the Eagles baseball team: practice every afternoon, games every Saturday. A busy summer. No time for the loneliness to creep up on him, for temptations to take hold. If he kept busy enough, he wouldn't think about a drink; he wouldn't think about Vicky.

It was past midnight when he let the dog outside for a few minutes. Father Don still hadn't come in, and he realized he'd been waiting for the other priest, half expecting the sounds of a motor cutting off in front, the front door opening. Surely, if the man had run into any trouble, he would have called.

He started up the stairs, bringing the phone from the

hall table as far as the cord would stretch. He set the phone on the top step. He would hear it ring, in case someone needed a priest in the middle of the night.

The sky was clear with the promise of sunshine when Father John walked back to the residence after the early-morning Mass. He always enjoyed the early Mass—the faithful parishioners scattered about the pews, murmuring the prayers, the first daylight blinking in the stained-glass windows.

The front door opened as he came up the steps. His assistant stood just inside, as if he'd been waiting for him. He had no idea when the man had gotten in last night. Late, he guessed, because he'd tossed about a long while, going over in his mind what he'd learned about Duncan Grover: a twenty-five-year-old man running from something, getting ready to start a job, trying to start over. And a girl in a convenience store whom he might never find. Hardly enough to convince a white detective to launch a homicide investigation.

And in the back of his mind, like the relentless beat of a drum, the words in the confessional: *There's gonna be more murders.*

"I have to talk to you," Father Don said, turning into the study.

Father John followed. "What is it?" His assistant had the blanched, drawn look of a man who'd been up all night.

"I'm gonna need a little time off."

"You okay?"

"I'm fine." Father Don jammed his fists into his khakis and began circling the study, an intent look in his eyes. "Just need a few days to myself. Thought I'd take a drive to the mountains. Find someplace to hide out awhile."

"Hide out?"

"Do some praying, thinking. Sometimes you have to get away. You know how it is."

He knew. He'd gone all the way to Boston a couple years ago and stayed two weeks. Still, Don Ryan had been here only a couple months.

"Does this have anything to do with Mary Ann Williams?" he asked.

The other priest yanked one hand from his pocket and waved it into the space between them. "Let's not turn this into a big deal, okay? I'm taking a few days off, that's all."

"What happened last night?" Father John persisted.

"Nothing happened." The other priest spit out the words. "I called one of Mary Ann's friends. She came over, and I stayed until the friend got her calmed down."

Father John walked over and sat down at his desk. His assistant was lying, and the man wasn't any better at it than dozens of people he'd counseled, dozens of penitents in the confessional—lying to themselves first, hoping that if someone else believed the lies, then they could also believe, as if the believing would make them true.

He glanced up. "Take whatever time you need. I'll be here when you get back, should you want to talk."

Fifteen minutes later—he'd just taken a spoonful of the oatmeal Elena had set before him—Father John heard the front door slam and, a moment after that, tires crunching the wet gravel on Circle Drive.

"Well, I told you so." Elena plunged a plate into the soapy water in the sink, disappointment etched in the set of her shoulders. Father John understood. Don Ryan wasn't just another priest in a passing parade. Here for a few weeks, a year, then moving on. He was . . . well, he'd seemed to like the place.

"What makes you think Father Don won't be back?" He heard the doubt creeping into his own voice.

"I told you before. He was never here," Elena said after a moment. "His spirit was somewhere else."

Father John finished the oatmeal. Considering. So many priests through the years. Elena *knew*. He was going to have to cut back on the summer programs, limit them to what he could handle. Until the Provincial found another assistant. He would be even busier than he'd imagined. Which meant he had even less time than he'd thought to convince Detective Slinger that Duncan Grover was murdered.

He thanked Elena for breakfast and asked her to tell anyone who stopped by that he'd be back later. Then he headed down the hallway, grabbed his jacket and cowboy hat, and left for Lander.

## ◀ 12 ▶

The Equitable Building spread over a quarter block at the corner of Seventeenth and Stout streets, massive stone towers with marble-paved floors and 1890s Tiffany stained-glass windows. Vicky found Baider Industries on the directory and rode the bronze-trimmed elevator up several floors.

She'd called this morning to make an appointment with Nathan Baider. The founder of Baider Industries may have turned the company over to his son, but the old man was still calling the shots, Wes had said. If anyone knew why Vince Lewis had wanted to see her, she suspected it would be Nathan Baider.

"Mr. Baider's schedule is full today." A woman's voice on the phone.

"Tell Mr. Baider I witnessed Vince Lewis's murder," she'd said.

"Murder!" A gasp burst over the line. "Mr. Lewis was in an unfortunate—"

She'd cut in: "Tell Mr. Baider what I said."

After a long pause the woman's voice had returned. "He'll see you right away."

Vicky emerged into another marble-paved vestibule and let herself through the glass doors across from the elevator. Instantly she was enveloped in the hushed silence of dark blue walls, clusters of chairs, and polished tables. Large photographs lined the walls on either side of a window that framed a view of the parking garage across the street.

"May I help you?" An attractive woman somewhere between thirty and fifty, with stylishly cut blond hair that brushed the collar of her red suit jacket, rose from behind the mahogany desk.

Vicky handed her a business card, which the woman studied for a couple of seconds, snapping the card between her red-tipped fingers. Finally she set the card down and said, "Wait here," letting herself through the door on the right.

Vicky strolled over to an arrangement of photographs behind the desk, western landscapes with white-peaked mountains and sunshine streaking the endless plains. Above the landscapes, the clear blue sky.

On each photo, small white arrows pointed to barely perceptible disruptions in the earth. She leaned closer, studying the areas beneath the arrows: gouges, clumps of buildings, roads flung through the wilderness, trucks, and bulldozers. She realized the photos had been shot from a great distance—from airplanes, maybe even satellites.

Beneath each photo was an engraved gold plate: CRIPPLE CREEK MINE, CANADA; JENNISON MINE, CANADA; and three mines in Wyoming—LEMLE, BRIDGER, KIMBERLY.

She crossed to the opposite wall. Here the landscape photos were replaced by photos of various-sized diamonds shimmering in the camera's flash. On the bottom frames were the identifying gold plates: THREE-CARAT YELLOW DIAMOND, KIMBERLY MINE, 1992. NINE-CARAT WHITE DIAMOND, BRIDGER MINE, 1993. SIX-CARAT BLUE DIAMOND, LEMLE MINE, 1996.

She strolled over to the glass-topped display case beneath the window. Flung out like grains of sand on a black velvet bed were dozens of diamonds. White, yellow, blue. Some as tiny as pinpricks, others as large as pebbles, all reflecting back the light and the colors in the room.

"They're synthetic."

Vicky swung around and faced the woman in the red suit.

"Synthetic?" She glanced again at the fiery stones. Was nothing what it seemed? Was everything a symbol of another reality?

The woman began explaining. The company could hardly keep millions of dollars in diamonds in the building. She gave a sharp laugh. What would the insurance company say? The stones were excellent cubic zirconia that could even fool a jeweler.

"The real diamonds are here." She gestured toward the photos behind her. "Baider Industries has an international reputation for the quality of the diamonds we produce. Notice all the gems have the four Cs required of excellent diamonds—color, cut, clarity, and estimable carat size. We've produced the largest finished diamond found in North America: fifteen-point-six carats." Slowly she took her eyes away. "Mr. Baider will see you now."

Vicky followed the woman down a corridor as wide as a small room. From beyond the closed doors came the muffled sounds of voices, a sharp burst of laughter.

"Mr. Baider has an important meeting in ten minutes." The woman paused at the last door. "Please be brief."

She ushered Vicky into a rectangular-shaped office that resembled the reception area with similar chairs and polished tables arranged around green plush carpeting, similar photos of landscapes and diamonds on the walls.

Nathan Baider sat behind a perfectly cleared desk,

hands folded on the shining surface. He looked more fit than she remembered, but she'd only spoken with him briefly at the emergency room. His cheeks and hands were sunburned and freckled, his gray hair tousled, as if he'd just come indoors. He wore a blue shirt and a dark tie somewhat askew, knotted in a hurry, she thought.

"Sit down," he said in a gravelly voice accustomed to obedience. The pale blue eyes didn't leave her as she crossed the office. She took the chair nearest to the desk. A few feet away, leaning against the wall, was a red-and-gold golf bag with the putter jammed halfway down. A minute earlier, she guessed, Nathan Baider had been putting a golf ball over the green carpet.

"Thank you for seeing me," she began.

He cut her off: "What's this about Vince being murdered?"

Vicky said, "I saw it happen. The black Camry deliberately ran him down."

Baider drew in a long breath that expanded the fronts of the blue shirt. "About thirty other people saw it happen, Detective Clark says, and nobody else calls it murder." He allowed the word to settle between them, his eyes steady on hers. "It was an accident, Ms. Holden. Some drunk weaving down the street, couldn't tell the curb from a white line. Hit-and-run, that's what it was."

"I was on my way to meet Mr. Lewis when he was killed," Vicky hurried on. There was little time. She half expected the secretary to appear and announce the meeting was over.

"Yes, yes." The man waved one hand over the desk. "So you informed me after the accident. If Vince made an appointment with you, it must have been personal business." He shrugged. "In any case, it no longer matters."

"It was a matter of life and death," Vicky said. "Someone killed him to keep him from talking to me."

Baider was quiet a long moment. He seemed to be staring at some image behind his eyes. "A very large assumption. What's your evidence, Ms. Holden?"

"Lewis's own words." She was thinking how she would demolish a witness on the stand for offering such evidence. *How can you be certain of what Mr. Lewis meant?* She hurried on: "Lewis's job was to locate new diamond deposits, am I correct?" Slowly now, feeling her way, groping to express the idea that had been nagging at her since she'd learned that Vince Lewis was dead. "Is it possible he located a diamond deposit on the Wind River Reservation?" It sounded preposterous, even as she spoke.

Baider shook his head. "You're correct about Lewis's job. We're always looking for kimberlite pipes that may be diamondiferous. Maybe you know the world market can no longer depend upon diamonds mined in Africa. Deposits in places like Angola, Congo, and Sierra Leone have been taken over by rebels. They've been flooding the world market with so-called conflict diamonds to finance their bloody wars. Damn conflict diamonds amounted to seven hundred million dollars a year until the industry got a certification program. Now diamonds traded on the world market gotta have certificates proving they didn't come from rebel-held mines. Not as easy as it sounds."

He shook his head and held up one hand, like a teacher about to make his point. "Much easier to certify diamonds mined in the United States. When we find a pipe, we file a claim. We have dozens of claims on the southern Wyoming border. The area is rich in diamond deposits. None in central Wyoming, I can assure you."

Slowly the man levered himself out of his chair. "I'm sure Lewis's accident was a great shock to you, Ms. Holden. I understand the urgency of your desire to find an explanation, but take some advice from a man who's knocked around a bit. Accidents happen. Sometimes nobody's to blame. Let it go, and put your mind to rest."

The door swung open and the woman in the red suit leaned into the office. "Your meeting, Mr. Baider," she said.

Vicky stood up, reached across the desk, and shook the man's hand. "Thank you for your time," she said. A waste of her own time, she was thinking. If what Baider said was true, there were no claims filed on the res, no records of any deposits. She was chasing phantoms. And yet, Vince Lewis had died trying to tell her something that affected her people.

She walked back through the office, the secretary's footsteps knocking behind her, and rode the elevator down. As the bronze doors parted, she spotted a younger version of Nathan Baider crossing the lobby—same height and build, same ruddy cheeks, tousled black hair that would be gray in a few years. Roz Baider, she guessed. The man was in a deep conversation with the stocky man beside him.

Suddenly Baider turned toward her. There was a flash of recognition in the man's eyes, and she wondered if Nathan had told him about her. For half a second she thought he might approach her. Instead, he resumed the conversation with the other man. They swung past a planter and walked hurriedly to the entrance, wing tips tapping out a staccato rhythm on the marble.

It struck her that neither Nathan Baider nor his son wanted her to know why Vince Lewis had called, but she had her own theory, and that theory was beginning to take on a strength beyond its likelihood. For a brief moment she allowed herself to wish that John O'Malley were here.

They could sit down together; she could test her theory against his logic. She considered calling him, then dismissed the idea. Not talking to him had made it seem easier to be so far away.

She dug through her black bag for her cell phone, dialed Laola, and asked her to check with the Wyoming Department of Environmental Quality for any authorizations given to Baider Industries to explore a diamond deposit in central Wyoming. Then she told the secretary to call Adam Elkman, the natural resources director on the reservation, and set up a phone interview as soon as possible. She would ask him if the company had requested permission to explore anywhere on the reservation. There was every possibility that Nathan Baider was lying. The company had *some* interest in the area. Otherwise, why had Vince Lewis tried to talk to her?

She stepped out onto Stout Street, dialing Steve Clark's number as she went. It surprised her when the detective picked up; she'd expected an answering service.

"I have to talk to you," she said, weaving through the business suits walking along the sidewalk.

"How about lunch?" There was an eagerness in the detective's voice that gave her a stab of discomfort. "One o'clock?" He named a restaurant in the Pavilions.

"I'll be there," she said.

# ◀ 13 ▶

Diners jammed the restaurant on the Sixteenth Street Mall, an assemblage of business suits in earnest conversations. Vicky spotted Steve Clark in a booth against the far wall. She waved away the maître d' and started through the maze of tables, snatching pieces of conversations as she went: . . . *stock options?* . . . *the new partner . . . close the deal.*

Steve caught her eye and jumped to his feet with the quick agility of a cowboy dismounting a horse. He was dressed in what she used to call his uniform: blue blazer over light blue shirt, subdued detective tie, tan slacks. Smiling at her. The laugh lines deepened at the corners of his eyes. One hand crunched a red napkin.

"You look beautiful." He waited until she'd settled across from him before resuming his own seat. The intense look in his eyes made her uncomfortable, aware of herself: the shoulder-length black hair, the dark, almond-shaped eyes, the tiny bump at the top of her nose—the Arapaho bump—the dark skin that had caused a few heads to follow her as she'd come through the restaurant.

A waiter in a white coat was sweeping about the table—welcome, welcome—pouring ice water, delivering menus. The sounds of tinkling ice cut through the buzz of conversations from nearby tables. After they'd ordered—club sandwich, pasta salad—Steve said, "It's good to have you back."

"Good to be here." The words rang hollow and superficial to her ears. She'd agreed to lunch; she hadn't considered that he might misconstrue her intentions. It had been a dozen years since they were undergraduates, two outsiders bumping into each other on the CU-Denver campus. He, fresh from a stint with the navy SEALs, and she, fresh from the reservation, the ink still wet on a divorce decree and two children back home with her mother.

"Here's to us," he said, lifting the water glass.

"Us?" There had never been "us."

"We're having lunch again. Just like old times."

"Here's to lunch," she said, clinking his glass.

"What made you leave Lander?" he said after a moment. "The shooting?"

Vicky leaned against the back cushion and waited until the waiter had set the pasta in front of her, the sandwich in front of Steve, then grated Parmesan over her plate with a cheeriness that struck a discordant note in the muted atmosphere that had settled over the table.

"How did you know?" she said when the waiter moved away.

"Reports come into the department." He shrugged and took a bite of his sandwich. After a moment he said, "Discharge of firearms resulting in death in the Rocky Mountain region. I snagged the report with your name in it."

"The man was about to shoot a friend of mine," she heard herself explaining. The same explanation she gave herself in the middle of the night when she couldn't sleep.

"Certainly justifiable, Vicky. Anyone would have done the same. Give yourself some time." He held her eyes a moment before taking another bite of the sandwich.

Vicky tried the pasta. It was lukewarm, with a congealed buttery taste. Finally she said, "What have you found out about the Lewis homicide?"

"What makes you so sure it's homicide?" He sounded mildly amused.

"I saw it happen, Steve."

"We don't know yet what caused the accident."

"I have a theory."

He set his sandwich down and regarded her. "Now, why doesn't that surprise me?"

"Listen, Steve," she began. "I believe it's possible that Baider Industries has located a diamond deposit on the reservation."

"Diamonds?" The amusement had changed into surprise. "That would have made the headlines."

"This is still the Old West," she said, keeping her voice low. "Prospectors still jump claims the way they used to jump the old gold and silver claims. Nathan Baider knows how the game is played. If his people located a new deposit, he'd keep it secret until he was ready to file a claim."

Steve pulled his mouth into a tight line of disapproval. A second passed. "You want me to buy a theory that Vince Lewis was killed because he was about to blow the whistle?"

"It makes sense." She struggled to ignore the questions in his eyes and hurried on before the theory she'd been constructing collapsed. "Baider could be waiting for a ruling on a very important case that's in the federal courts, *Navajo Nation* v. *Lexcon*." She explained the district court ruling. How the tribes didn't necessarily own the methane gas on their lands. How the ruling was a wedge other companies could use to claim that tribes might not have total control of other natural resources on reservations. How Baider could claim the Arapahos and Shoshones on the Wind River Reservation didn't control any diamond deposits. She told him she was working on the appeal. *The Navajos had to appeal.* "Baider could be waiting to file a claim, hoping he won't have to pay royalties."

"If what you say is true"—the detective was shaking his head—"Lewis would come in for a share of the profits. Why blow the whistle?"

Vicky sat back against the booth. She didn't have the answer. She could feel the theory starting to crumble, as if the ground were giving way beneath her feet.

"Look," he said in a conciliatory tone, "you could be right. Maybe it was homicide. We won't know until we find the driver."

"What about the license?"

"Lifted from a Chevy van at the airport," he said. "Oldest trick in the book, Vicky. Some guy wants to cover his tracks, so he cruises the outlying lots. Security's not as close. Anybody knows his business can lift a pair of plates in about two minutes. Salesman got back from Florida and didn't know he was driving without plates until the state patrol pulled him over on I-70. You'd be surprised how many people drive out of lots without checking to see if they still have plates."

Vicky felt a little surge of excitement. "So, whoever killed Lewis went to a lot of trouble to make the car untraceable," she said. "Someone at Baider could have arranged for a killer to run Lewis down before our meeting. That explains why the Camry came out of nowhere. The killer was waiting somewhere down the block."

"Whoa, hold on there." Steve set his own cup down. Brown liquid sloshed into the saucer. "You're like an eighteen-wheeler runaway coming off the mountain. First rule in an investigation, don't get married to one theory. The guy driving the Camry could've lifted the plates for some other reason. A burglary, or a drug deal. His mind's on the big deal coming down when he jumps the curb and hits a pedestrian who happens to be Vince Lewis."

"You believe that?" Vicky made no effort to stifle the astonishment in her voice.

"Until we find the driver"—he held her gaze—"anything's possible. We're running a check on recent arrests and complaints. We'll see if a black Camry figures in any other reported crimes. And we're following some other leads." He tapped his fingers on the table, as if he was trying to make up his mind how much to divulge. "Turns out Lewis's wife, Jana, served him with divorce papers three days before he was killed," he said finally. "Alleged infidelity. Could be Lewis was looking for a good divorce lawyer when he called you."

She didn't believe it. A man like Lewis could hire the best divorce lawyer on Seventeenth Street. When she didn't say anything, the detective went on: "The widow gave us the names of a couple of Lewis's girlfriends. We interviewed them. Seemed pretty broken up by the guy's death, but you never know. One could have wanted to settle an old score."

He lifted his cup and took a long sip, regarding her over the rim for a long moment. Then he set the cup down. "Turns out the grieving widow is due to collect on a big insurance policy. Three mil. Could be she wanted to make sure Lewis didn't have time to change the beneficiary."

Vicky glanced around the restaurant—waiters hovering over tables, diners getting to their feet. Her theory could still be right. Lewis had called *her,* an Arapaho attorney. She brought her gaze back. "I heard Roz Baider was taking over the company. How did that affect Lewis?"

Steve let out a long sigh. "Don't you ever give up?"

The buzz of conversation, the sound of glass tinkling, drifted between them a moment. Finally he said in a lowered voice, "Lewis climbed the ladder to vice-president of development and Nathan Baider's right-hand man in only three years. He was hard-driving and ambitious. A profile that would probably fit a lot of guys in this dining room." He nodded at the tables stretching toward the maître d's station. Some were empty now.

"Nobody knows what'll happen when another man takes the chief's seat, but Roz made it sound like Lewis would be part of the reorganization."

"Reorganization?"

Steve shrugged. "Wouldn't be the first time a son decided he could do things better."

Vicky sat quietly for a moment, only half-aware of the flashes of white jackets bobbing past. "Suppose," she began, "that Lewis wasn't going to be part of the reorganized company. Maybe he'd want to blow the whistle about a secret diamond deposit."

Steve was shaking his head. "Sweetheart, you've been watching too many detective shows." He leaned over the table, so close she could smell the mustard and coffee on his breath. "Nobody at Baider Industries mentioned anything about Lewis being out. Just the opposite. He was the brains. Roz needed the man."

Vicky felt a longing to be back in Lander, at the café on Main Street, John O'Malley across from her, examining her theory piece by piece, looking for the logical pattern. There was always a pattern.

The waiter appeared with a small black folder, and Vicky dug in her bag for a couple of bills, which Steve waved away. "It's been a long time since you had lunch with me." He slipped a credit card into the folder. "Look, Vicky," he said, "I understand your worry. I'll have another talk with senior and junior Baider. Maybe they forgot to mention a diamond deposit on the res."

"Will you let me know what you find out?"

He was signing the charge slip, collecting his card. He looked up. "I'll let you know."

They slid out of the booth at the same moment, and he ushered her through the maze of tables and into the courtyard that connected the Pavilions' shops to the Sixteenth Street mall. She could feel the firm pressure of his hand on the small of her back as they walked down the concrete steps to the sidewalk.

"I'd like to see you, Vicky," he said, guiding her to one side, away from the crowd. The shuttle swooshed along the mall.

"As soon as you find out—"

"Forget the Lewis case a minute. You're unattached, right?" He didn't wait for a response. "So am I. So what's wrong with two unattached people, a beautiful woman and a so-so guy, getting together?"

Vicky raised one hand, but before she could say anything, he said, "You know I've been attracted to you since you bumped into me on campus. That was deliberate, right?" He grinned.

"Deliberate?"

"You saw me coming through the door. Next thing I know, I'm picking up your papers and notes all over the stairs. You got my attention all right."

Vicky threw her head back and laughed. "It could've been an orangutan coming through the door, Steve. I wasn't looking where I was going."

A small shadow of pain crossed his face.

"I'm very glad it was you," she said hurriedly. "You

did such a good job of getting all of my notes before they blew away, and—" She paused. "You've been a good friend."

"How about having dinner with a good friend?"

Vicky looked away. A trio of men in dark suits glanced at them as they passed by. She'd been thinking about John O'Malley all during lunch, she realized. He had never said to her "have dinner with me."

"You were right earlier," she said, bringing her eyes back. "I'm still running from what happened on the res." She saw in his expression that he thought she meant the shooting. "I need some time."

"I've been waiting a long time. I can wait a little longer." He made a halfhearted attempt at a shrug.

She was about to turn away when his hand reached out and touched her shoulder, holding her lightly in place. "Promise me you'll stay out of this investigation, Vicky. If it is homicide and the guy who killed Lewis thinks you're trying to find out why, he could come after you."

"I promise not to do anything rash," she said.

"Don't do anything at all." A note of sternness in his voice.

She smiled, then slipped past him and joined the knots of people on the sidewalk. She waited for another shuttle to glide past, trailing pneumatic sounds, then started across the bricked pathway, only half-aware of his eyes following her. She was thinking that a woman who had filed for divorce might be willing to talk about her husband's activities at Baider Industries.

# ◄ 14 ►

Detective Matt Slinger might have been a professional wrestler, Father John thought. The fleshy, pushed-in face, the nose that looked as if it had been broken once or twice, the thick mane of dark hair. He crossed the waiting room at the Fremont County Sheriff's Department and extended his hand. "Father O'Malley," he said. His smile was friendly and guarded. His grip hard. "Come on back." He gestured toward the door he'd just come through.

Father John followed the man down a corridor with fluorescent light washing over the gray walls and pebbled-glass doors. They emerged into a room the size of a large conference room. Papers and folders had been spread over the surfaces of three desks pushed against one wall in no particular order that Father John could see. Bookcases stuffed with folders, boxes, and books ran along the opposite wall. Across the room, rain spattered the two windows that framed a blurred view of the cars and trucks in the parking lot.

"Have a seat." The detective pushed a chair over to one of the desks, then took the barrel-shaped chair on the other side. Leaning back, he said, "So you're the Indian priest

I've heard about. Gotten yourself mixed up in a few homicides around here."

"Not by choice, I assure you." Father John sat down
and laid his cowboy hat on the tiled floor next to his feet.
It always surprised him: Indian priest. He was an Irish-
man, from Boston, assigned to St. Francis Mission. He
happened to like it there.

The detective's mouth turned up in amusement. "You
think Duncan Grover's death was another one of your
homicides?" That was what Father John had told him
when he'd called to make an appointment.

"It's a possibility." He was treading a fine line. All that
he *knew* he'd heard in the confessional. The rest was theory, with no evidence to back it up.

"You a friend of the victim's?" The detective rearranged his bulky frame and folded his hands over his
stomach.

Father John admitted he'd never met the man.

"Friend of the family?"

"No."

"Then what makes you think somebody killed him?"

"I've been talking to people on the res," Father John
began, lining up his argument in a logical order. "Ben
Holden told me Grover went to the Arapaho Ranch looking for a job. He agreed to hire him in a couple of weeks.
A man planning to kill himself doesn't go job hunting."

The detective shifted again. "Stranger things have happened."

"Look, Detective," Father John said, taking a different
tack, "Holden believes Grover was in some kind of trouble in Denver. Somebody could have followed him here
and killed him."

"Oh, Grover was in trouble, all right." A slow smile
burned through the detective's face. "Had a robbery war-

rant out on him in Colorado. He'd been working construction jobs for a temp agency. Had quite a scam stealing jackhammers and compressors and stuff that he could sell for decent cash. The foreman at the last job got onto him and filed a complaint. Grover already had two convictions. Third strike, and he was looking at prison for a very long time. So he took off and came to the res, the way Indians like to do. Minute they get into trouble in the big white world, they come running home."

"Grover was from Oklahoma." Father John didn't try to conceal his irritation.

"Wind River is Indian country." The man was warming to the subject now. "Looks up Ben Holden, plays the good Indian, goes to stay with a holy man and learn Indian ways, hoping nobody'll notice him."

"And kills himself? Come on, Detective. You're describing a man who wanted to live."

"Not in prison, he didn't. You ask me, Grover had one strong motive to kill himself." He hunched forward. "Another thing, Father O'Malley, there's no evidence of anybody else on that ledge at the time of death."

Father John glanced at the rain-smeared windows. The room was muggy and warm. He had to concede that what the detective said made sense. There was a certain logic to it. He might even have believed it if it hadn't been for the man in the confessional.

He said, "Grover may have a girlfriend in the area." It was a gamble. He had no proof that the woman who had called Gus Iron Bear was Grover's girlfriend. "She might be able to tell you if Grover was running from somebody."

"What girlfriend?"

Father John told him about his conversation with Gus. The detective seemed to consider this. Finally he said,

"Could've been anybody, Father. Some girl he met in a bar. If she was involved with the guy, why hasn't she come forward, told us whatever she knows?"

"Maybe she's scared. Maybe she doesn't want to talk to the police."

"Maybe she doesn't know anything." A flush of impatience came into the detective's cheeks.

Father John pushed on: "Duncan Grover was trying to start over, put the past behind, follow a different road. No Indian's going to kill himself on a vision quest in a sacred place like Bear Lake. It would be a sacrilege, an offense to the spirits."

"I know all about Indian vision quests." The detective plopped one hand onto a stack of papers. A couple of sheets slid across the desk. "Grover was up there on that high ledge for three days without food or water, smoking a pipe and breathing in that sage they like to burn. After a while he got up the courage to throw himself off the cliff."

"It didn't happen." Father John's tone had a harder edge than he'd intended.

Matt Slinger lifted his other hand and rubbed his fingers into his temple, as if to rub away a minor annoyance. "Okay, Father O'Malley. Have it your way. Maybe he was in some kind of altered state of consciousness and didn't realize that he couldn't fly like an eagle. Maybe that's what happened. It comes down to the same thing. Duncan Grover was responsible for his own death, which makes it suicide."

Father John felt as if he were running into brick walls. There had to be another way. He drew in a long breath and began again: "What kind of injuries did he have?"

"The lethal kind." The detective's gaze was steady. A half second passed before he reached for a file folder, flipped it open, and began shuffling through the official-looking forms.

Father John realized the detective had been expecting the question. He'd already retrieved Grover's file from a filing cabinet.

"Multiple contusions, bruises." Slinger spoke in a monotone of futility. "Broken ribs, femurs, arms. Spinal cord crushed." He glanced up. "Shall I go on?"

"What about his skull?"

"Crushed left temporal."

That was it, the opening he'd been looking for. He said: "Isn't it possible that Grover was struck in the head, then thrown off the ledge?"

Slinger gave a sharp expulsion of breath that passed for a laugh. "Speculation's cheap, Father O'Malley," he said. "Fact is, Grover fell two hundred feet off a cliff, bounced through some sharp boulders, which accounts for his injuries. Take my word, he decided that dying on a vision quest was more honorable than rotting in prison."

The detective set both palms against the desk and pushed himself to his feet. "I suggest you forget about trying to turn Grover's suicide into something it wasn't. The guy was a loser. He decided to end his life. It's as simple as that. Why don't you just remember him in your prayers."

Father John picked up his hat and got to his feet. There was a loud clap of thunder, then the glow of lightning in the window. Outside the rain was beating on the asphalt parking lot. He said: "How do you know somebody else won't be killed?"

"What're you talking about?"

He kept his eyes on the other man's. He was talking about what he'd heard in the confessional—the sealed confessional. "If you're wrong," he said, "there's a killer in the area. He could kill again."

Slinger glanced away. Rubbing at his temple again. Finally he looked back. "I need the girlfriend's name, Father O'Malley. Give me a name. I'll find her and have a talk with her."

A surge of hope, like lightning. For the first time since the man had come into the confessional, Father John felt there was a chance that Duncan Grover's killer would be found. That nobody else would have to die. A name, and Detective Slinger would continue the investigation.

Father John set his cowboy hat on his head and headed down the corridor. There was a girl somewhere in Lander who knew Duncan Grover. A girl who'd left a message for him to call her at the convenience store. Which could mean—he could almost taste the certainty of it—that she worked at one of the convenience stores.

He let himself out through the glass-door entrance and, hunching his shoulders in the rain, ran across the lot to the Toyota. He'd start with the convenience stores on Main Street.

# ‹ 15 ›

Father John waited for a semi to pass on Main Street before he took a left into the parking lot between a motel and convenience store. It was his second stop. The rain banged on the Toyota's roof, nearly drowning out the sounds of *Faust*. He turned off the tape player and ran across the pavement to the double glass doors with posters plastered on the inside: CARTON CIGARETTE—$22.99; TODAY'S SPECIAL—SIX-PACK COKE, $1.29.

He stepped inside and stopped. Behind the counter: a small, black-haired woman, about twenty, eyes like slate, golden-brown skin, sharp cheekbones, and the small bump in her nose—the nose of the Arapaho. Several customers waited in line, gripping packages of Twinkies, cans of pop, candy bars. He walked down the center aisle and selected an apple from the bin on the rear wall, a Coke from the cooler, and wandered back to the register. One customer now—an elderly woman with a pink plastic hat clamped over her head and a clear plastic coat hanging loosely over a dark sweatsuit.

The young woman behind the counter handed the customer some coins and reached for the items he was holding. Her hair was pulled back, caught with a pink beaded barrette—the way Vicky sometimes wore her hair. An unimportant detail—a pink barrette, for God's sake—and she was in his mind as though she'd never left.

The young woman ran the Coke bottle over the scanner and tapped in some numbers on the register. "One-oh-seven," she said.

He fished some coins out of his blue jeans pocket and pushed them across the counter. "Are you a friend of Duncan Grover's?" he said.

She flinched, as if he'd struck her.

She was the one he was looking for, he was certain. Her hand was suspended over the coins, her dark eyes darted about. "Who wants to know?" she said in a voice tight with fear and hostility.

"I'm Father O'Malley. From the reservation."

She was staring at him. The cowboy hat, the rain slicker, the blue jeans.

"Yeah, and I'm Annette Funuchio."

"Funicello."

"Whatever." She punched open the cash register, scooped up the coins, and dropped them inside. Eyes still darting about the store. The cash register drawer slammed shut. The coolers hummed into the silence behind him, and a veil of rain covered the windows.

"I'd like to talk to you about Duncan." He picked up the apple and Coke.

The woman swallowed twice, looking about frantically now, eyes bright with fear.

"There's no need to be afraid," he said.

"What do you want?"

"I believe your friend was murdered."

She drew in her lower lip and crossed her arms over her white T-shirt, hugging herself, fingers plucking at her sleeves. "Can't you see I'm working?"

"When do you get off?"

"You don't look like a priest." Her gaze traveled to the cowboy hat he'd pushed back on his head.

He removed the wallet from his back pocket, took out his driver's license, and slid it across the counter.

She peered down over crossed arms. "John O'Malley, SJ." She raised her eyes and stared at him with a mixture of curiosity and wariness. "SJ?"

"Society of Jesus. I'm a Jesuit priest."

He replaced the license and jammed his wallet back into his pocket. "I can wait until you get off."

An argument was playing out behind the black eyes. "I'm supposed to take a break in ten minutes when the manager gets back," she said finally. "There's a picnic table out back. I'll meet you outside."

It's raining outside, he thought. He said, "I'll be waiting."

He walked around the brick building, staying close to the wall. Water gushed off the overhang and splashed onto the sidewalk. The picnic table and two benches stood on a concrete slab in the rear, facing a solid wood fence that marked the backyards of adjoining houses. There was a scattering of pickups in the parking lot on the right, shallow rivers running around the tires. He straddled a bench, popped open the Coke, and bit into the apple. The rain sounded like an army of small birds pecking the corrugated overhang. An engine backfired in the lot.

He'd finished both the Coke and apple by the time she dodged around the corner. She was bundled in a puffy red jacket, which she hugged to herself, one front lapping the other. She sank onto the bench across from him and began tugging at a pocket in her jacket, finally extracting a package of cigarettes. She shook one out. Another tug for a lighter, which she flicked a couple of times, cupping the flame. The light danced in her dark eyes.

Throwing her head back, she blew out a strand of smoke and held the package toward him.

Father John shook his head. The smell of the smoke brought back a memory of whiskey and stuffy bars and the forced conviviality and mindless banter that, for a few hours, had once obscured the loneliness. He swallowed back the memory. It was not one he wanted.

"What's your name?" he said.

She hesitated, took a long drag on the cigarette. "Ali," she said finally, smoke curling from her nostrils. "Ali Burris. Why should I tell you about Duncan?"

"Because I'm trying to convince Detective Slinger to reopen the investigation."

She blew out a ring of smoke and watched it dissolve into the rain. "I don't get it. A white man that gives a shit about some Indian? Slinger and the coroner already made up their minds that Duncan killed himself."

He leaned toward her. "I'm trying to change their minds."

"Yeah, you'd do that. You being a priest." She took another drag from the cigarette and looked away.

"Maybe," he said. He liked to believe that even if he weren't a priest, if he'd never come to St. Francis Mission, he would still care about justice. "A man doesn't look for a job, go on a vision quest, then kill himself."

Slowly she brought her eyes back to his, and he realized that she did have the answers. He only had to ask the right questions. "Tell me about Duncan," he said.

"Paranoid. Crazy." She threw her head back, her gaze following the smoke. "What else you want to know?"

"Why don't you start at the beginning?"

"The beginning? My break's only fifteen minutes."

"You met him in Denver?"

"Yeah." She flipped the ash at the end of the cigarette

and gazed at the parking lot, summoning the memory. "Six months ago at a bar. We got together, you could say."

"Where did he work?"

"Construction jobs, different places." She looked back. "When he worked, that is. Duncan's real work was ripping off the construction sites. Helped himself to a lot of power tools. Always after the big score, that was Duncan." A half smile faded into a blank look of acceptance. "He'd make a couple hundred bucks, get drunk, go broke again. So he'd go back to the temp agency, and they'd find him another job. The thing was, Duncan was a damn good worker when he wanted to work."

She stared at the cigarette. "A real con man, Duncan. Sure as hell conned me. Lived at my apartment, took my money. God, what a fool I was."

"You said he was paranoid," Father John prodded.

"Yeah, well, I guess he had reason, didn't he? Somebody offed him."

"Who do you think killed him?" Father John felt the sense of anticipation that often came over him during counseling sessions, in the confessional, in the archives, researching history—the sense that the truth was about to announce itself.

Ali Burris tossed the cigarette butt into a puddle. It made a sizzling noise. "The guys he was stiffing got onto him," she said. "Bunch of lowlifes, stealing stuff and cheating each other."

"Wait a minute. You're saying somebody killed Duncan because he held out on them? What are we talking about? A few hundred dollars?"

"You don't know these guys, Father. They'd kill you for a pack of cigarettes. I said to Duncan, we gotta get outta Denver, but he didn't want to leave. So I said, I'm gone." She kept her eyes on his. "I was scared of those creeps."

"Did they threaten you?"

"Did they threaten me?" Her voice rose in astonishment. "They didn't have to threaten me. I knew they'd beat the hell outta me if I ever opened my mouth about 'em." She threw a nervous glance at the parking lot. "I took off and came here. I got an aunt on the res. Figured I could lay low for a while."

"How'd Duncan find you?"

She looked away, smoothed back the black hair, reclasped the beaded barrette. After a moment she said, "I called him after a couple weeks. I mean, it wasn't exactly Duncan I was trying to get away from. It was the other guys. He said he was ready to get away, too, and start over. So he come up here."

"Did he come alone?"

She nodded, then let her gaze roam over the parking lot. "I thought things was gonna be different . . ." she began, her voice quiet. "They was as bad as before."

"Why, Ali? Did someone follow him?" He was close now. The truth was here.

She lifted her head. There was a smudge of mascara on her cheek. "Yeah, they came after him. I never should've let him stay with me. Crazy fuckhead. All the time keeping the shutters closed, living in the dark like some kinda animal. Peering through the slats. 'There goes Eddie,' he'd say. 'There goes Jimmie.' I'd run over to the window, but nobody was there. Just the empty street."

The rain was coming harder, and the wind blew sprays of water that carried the odors of wet asphalt and garbage. The girl went on: she'd told Duncan to get himself straightened out. Get a job. Go on a vision quest. The tears welled in her eyes and ran down her cheeks in thin black lines. "One of them creeps got him up there at Bear Lake."

"Help me," he said. "Give me the name."

"I don't know."

"You do know, Ali." He reached out and laid a hand on the puffy jacket sleeve.

"He killed Grover. He's gonna kill me, too." The words came in a long wail. She yanked her arm away, jumped to her feet, and ran around the corner of the building.

He went after her, grabbed her arm, and swung her toward him. She was so light, it surprised him. A child trembling inside the puffy jacket. "Ali, I'm trying to help you. Who killed Grover?"

She tried to pull away, but he held on, and she stared up at him for several seconds, a mixture of fear and resignation behind her eyes. Finally the words came, like water breaking over a dam. His name was Eddie. She didn't know his last name. A Pueblo Indian from New Mexico. Duncan and him got together at the Denver Indian Center. He was crazier than Duncan, but Duncan was gonna make a big score off him. One last score. Then they were gonna come up here and start over, just her and Duncan.

"I want you to tell this to Detective Slinger." Father John kept his hand on her arm. He could sense the impulse to run, like an electric spark firing inside her.

"Tell the police? You're as whacked as Duncan. What d'ya think's gonna happen to me if I blow the whistle on Eddie? He's still hanging around. I know it! I seen his brown truck on Main Street last night. He could be waiting for the right time to get me, like he did Duncan. Oh, God. Why am I talking to you?" She tried to wrench herself free again.

He let her go, but this time she didn't take off running.

"You shouldn't be alone, Ali," he said. "Go to the res and stay with your aunt. Take a few days off." He nodded toward the brick wall.

"A few days off?" Contempt and incredulity flowed into her expression. "And then I get fired and don't have a job. And my auntie's got enough problems without me showing up with no money and some Indian after me." She glanced past the parking lot to the traffic flowing along Main Street.

A chill ran through him. What had he done? Eddie could drive by, spot her talking to a white man in a cowboy hat—a cop, maybe. And she, the only one who could identify a murderer.

"Listen, Ali," he said. She had started walking, and he stayed with her. "Tell your boss you need time off for an emergency. There's a guest house at the mission. You can stay there until Detective Slinger picks up Eddie. You'll be safe."

"Leave me alone." She surged ahead and broke into a run, slipping on the wet pavement, weaving between the brick wall and the bumpers of the parked cars.

By the time he reached the front, she was nowhere in sight, and he wondered if she'd ducked into the convenience store or kept running. Where? Where could she go that Eddie wouldn't find her?

He slid into the Toyota and turned the ignition. The engine choked into life. He drove onto Main Street and headed north. A few minutes later he was speeding down Highway 789, the wind driving the rain over the hood of the pickup, wipers swinging across the windshield.

He replayed the conversation in his mind again and again. A man named Eddie staying in the area to kill anyone who could link him to Duncan Grover. Another man, Jimmie. The witness. The penitent.

It didn't add up. Something was missing, but he couldn't figure out what it was. If Eddie intended to kill Ali Burris, why hadn't he done so by now? The girl was easy to find—he'd found her right away. What was Eddie waiting for? He could have killed Grover, then disappeared into New Mexico, into the Pueblos. Why was he still here?

Father John slowed past the flat storefronts and restaurants of Hudson, then sped up again on Rendezvous Road. There was no other traffic, only the rainswept plains stretching into the distances. A new idea began to form in his mind. What was it the man had said in the confessional? Something about the boss wanting to teach the Indian to mind his own business.

Maybe Eddie hadn't killed Grover for revenge after all. Maybe there was some other reason, something that Ali Burris didn't know about.

He turned east on Seventeen Mile Road, mentally ticking off his options. He could talk to Slinger again. He rejected the idea. What proof did he have? A confession that he couldn't talk about. The stammered words of a girl scared out of her mind. Ali Burris would never tell the detective what she'd told him, and without her he had nothing.

Except—the name of a murderer.

By the time he turned into the mission grounds, he knew what he had to do. He was going to have to find a man called Eddie who didn't want to be found.

He drove down the straightaway lined with cottonwoods that moved lazily in the rain. As he turned onto Circle Drive, he saw Father Don's blue sedan parked in front of the administration building.

# ‹ 16 ›

Father John parked next to the sedan and hurried inside. Down the corridor, past the door to his own office, a mixture of surprise and foreboding taking hold of him. Some part of him, he realized, hadn't expected Father Don to return.

He stopped at the opened door at the far end of the corridor. Papers stacked neatly on the desk; books upright in the bookcases, as if Father Don had just stepped away.

He retraced his steps to his own office and sank into the leather chair with creases and folds that matched the contours of his own body. He reached for the phone. The other priest was probably at the residence. He was about to dial the number when he noticed the flashing light on the answering machine. He set the receiver down and pushed the button.

"Todd Hartley at the *Gazette*." The voice was unfamiliar. "Like to talk with you as soon as possible."

Father John jotted down the number the voice rattled off, wondering what the reporter wanted. He could have talked to Slinger, heard that the pastor at St. Francis wasn't buying the suicide verdict on Duncan Grover.

A whirring noise on the machine, then the voice of

Father Bill Rutherford, the Provincial: "Call me, John. It's very important."

Father John swiveled around and stared out the window at the rain. So Elena was right. Don Ryan was leaving, and the Provincial was about to deliver the usual promise: no need to worry; another man on the way. As soon as he could find another Jesuit eager to spend time on an Indian reservation. In the meantime . . .

In the meantime, he'd be alone. People streaming through the office, telephone ringing, sick people to visit, meetings to attend. Even with an assistant, he was always behind.

He tried to shake off the foreboding. He was jumping to conclusions. Father Don had returned, a good sign the man might stay awhile. He was probably over at the residence, eating a sandwich, visiting with Elena.

Before he returned the calls, he wanted to check out Eddie. He picked up the phone, dialed information, and got the number for Howard and Fergus in Denver. A couple of seconds passed, and he had Vicky's voice mail. "Please leave your name and number . . ."

She was five hundred miles away, and the reality brought a mixture of longing and reprieve. He was a priest; he wanted to keep his vows. Temptation was easier to overcome when it was five hundred miles away.

He told her voice mail that he was trying to find a Pueblo Indian named Eddie who could be involved in the recent death of a man named Duncan Grover. A so-called suicide. Someone at the Denver Indian Center might know Eddie. Anything she could find out would help. He ended by saying he hoped everything was well, then disconnected the call, not trusting himself to say more.

Next he dialed the Provincial's office, aware of the

muscles across his shoulders clenching against the possible bad news.

"Father Rutherford." The voice interrupted the first ring.

"John, returning your call." At the seminary twenty years before—a lifetime ago—they'd been friends. "What's going on?"

"You haven't heard?" Disbelief edged the Provincial's tone.

Now the tension was like fists gripping his shoulders. "You'd better fill me in."

"A lawsuit's been filed against the Province, the Society, the Archdiocese of Milwaukee, and St. Francis Mission."

"Lawsuit! What are you talking about?"

"I'm afraid Don Ryan's been unjustly accused—"

"Don Ryan?"

"—unjustly accused of sexual misconduct toward a young woman—"

Father John cut in: "Mary Ann Williams."

"You know her, then?"

"I've met her." His throat felt tight with anger.

"She's hired lawyers who think Catholic priests are a bunch of perverts and sexual predators. They've won some big cases with a few bad apples." A sigh of weariness floated over the line. "Show me the organization that doesn't have bad apples. Anyway, the lawyers have filed a lawsuit charging Don Ryan—a fine priest, excellent teacher with an unblemished record—with manipulative and sexually opportunistic conduct and breach of fiduciary duty and a lot of other legal jargon. Our lawyers are working on the complaint, but we may have to see this through to trial."

"Suppose she wins?" Father John could still see the

young woman running down the steps of the administration building.

"She's asking a million and a half. Since she claims the misconduct continued at the mission, St. Francis would have to pay its share. She's demanding punitive damages for post traumatic stress disorder plus loss of income after she quit her job in Milwaukee and moved to Riverton. If we lose, our insurance will pay part, but we'll still have to sell some of the mission land, perhaps the strip along the highway."

Father John looked back at the window, the rain sweeping through the cottonwoods, blurring the field where the Eagles practiced. Anger smoldered inside him like a wildfire ready to break out, and once started, he knew, hard to control. How dare Don Ryan put the mission at risk! It belonged to the Arapahos. They had laid the stone in the buildings, set the steeple on the church, painted the symbols on the walls. It was only a legal technicality that, more than a century ago, the chiefs had asked the Jesuits to come and educate the children and had given the Jesuits enough land for a mission.

He tried to focus on what the Provincial was saying, something about Don Ryan being distraught, going back to Milwaukee for a retreat.

"We should offer to settle, Bill," Father John said.

"Settle? I'll take that as a momentary lapse in your judgment. The woman's lying, impugning the character of a fine priest. Our lawyers assure us we'll win at trial, that a jury won't believe her. There's no proof that he coerced her in any way."

"What's that supposed to mean?"

"Two consenting adults, John. There was no taking advantage of."

"We both know that makes no difference. If he was

counseling her, that sets up a special relationship. The victim can't consent."

"The woman should still accept the consequences of her own actions."

The front door opened and shut, sending a blast of cool air through the office. Don Ryan stepped into the doorway, his face lost in the shadows of his slicker hood.

"Couple more things." There was a sharp tone of authority in the Provincial's voice. "Our lawyer will be in Riverton day after tomorrow to interview you. "I'd also like you to refer any media questions to me. Understand?"

He understood. Todd Hartley from the *Gazette* already had the news. Now he wanted a statement from the pastor at St. Francis. Father John dropped the receiver in the cradle.

"Sit down," he said to the man in the doorway.

The other priest pushed the hood back, came across the office, and dropped into a side chair, like a penitent, eyes puffy and red, dark lines etching the corners of his mouth.

"I take it you've heard." He threw up both hands in a kind of supplication. "I'm afraid I let myself get carried away back in Milwaukee, didn't use the soundest judgment. There was a brief"—he swallowed—"encounter that didn't mean—"

"Don't bullshit me."

The other priest's head snapped back. He stared at him a moment, some kind of debate going on behind the red-rimmed eyes. Finally he said, "I fell in love with her."

"Why didn't you tell the Provincial the truth?"

Don Ryan dropped his gaze to the floor. "What difference would it make? I have no intention of leaving the priesthood. A priest forever, according to the Order of Melchizedek and all that."

"Is that what you told Mary Ann Williams before she followed you here?"

The sound of the rain outside crowded into the space between them. After a moment the other priest said, "I couldn't stand the thought of losing her. You know what I'm talking about." He looked up, locking eyes with him. "Your reputation isn't as pure as snow," he said. "You're not exactly known as Saint John O'Malley around the Province. There's a lot of speculation about you and the Arapaho lawyer lady."

Father Don shifted forward. "Why don't *you* stop bullshitting *me* with your high-and-mighty attitude? The only difference between us is that Mary Ann decided to sue me."

Father John rose out of his chair, and the other priest shot to his feet. Leaning over the desk, Father John said, "I don't care what you've heard; you've got it wrong." He stopped himself from trying to explain the truth. What was the truth? That he and Vicky never had an affair? No promises made? That was only part of the truth. What about the unspoken promises, the longing, the immense sense of loss when she'd left? He didn't take his eyes away from the other man's. It was a thin line that divided them.

"Tell the Provincial you want to settle," he said.

"I can't do that."

"You said you love her."

"I have a career, a reputation."

Father John gripped the edge of the desk, aware of his knuckles popping white through his skin. "You'd better get out," he said.

He stayed at his desk a long time, until the rain had stopped and darkness had begun to creep outside the window, until he heard the engine in the blue sedan turn over and saw the vehicle swing around Circle Drive, headlights flashing past.

Still he waited, bolted in place by the realization that he might have put St. Francis at risk himself. His throat was as dry as sandpaper. He wanted a drink. One drink, and he would be calmer, he knew. But there was no alcohol at the mission, and he was grateful for that.

Finally he got up and walked over to the window. The mission was as peaceful in the rain as an Arapaho village in the Old Time. He would not call Vicky again, he resolved, and he wondered how he would keep the resolve. Temptation is strong—how often he'd said the words to penitents—but God's grace is stronger. He would find Eddie on his own. The man was out there somewhere in the grayness that spread beyond the mission.

He went back to the desk, dialed the reporter's number, and left a message. "Father John O'Malley. I'm on my way to Lander to talk with you."

# ‹ 17 ›

Traffic crawled down Main Street, splashing water over the cars and pickups parked at the curb. It had stopped raining, but moisture hung in the air like a faint memory. Father John found a parking spot a half block past the redbrick building that housed the *Gazette* offices and walked back along the storefronts. The smell of fresh grass mingled with the odors of exhaust and gasoline.

Just inside the front door was a tiled lobby, plastic chairs on each side, a counter directly ahead. The silver-haired woman behind the counter looked up from an opened newspaper and regarded him over half-moon glasses. "Father O'Malley," she said, drawing in a long breath that expanded her ample chest. "What can we do for you?"

"Good to see you." He recognized her—third pew from the back, ten o'clock Sunday Mass, four or five times a year. Once she'd caught him outside after Mass and pumped his hand for several seconds, assuring him that if there was ever anything the *Gazette* could do for his Indians, he had only to ask. Well, he was here to ask.

*Refer any media to me.* Bill Rutherford's voice still echoed in his head. Well, not exactly. The Provincial had said, "I'd like you to refer any media to me." It was a preference, not an order. He smiled at the slight Jesuitical difference.

"Todd Hartley in?" he said to the woman.

"I'll check." She flashed a reassuring smile, as though the fact that it was close to quitting time made no difference, and reached for the phone. "Father O'Malley to see you," she said. Then: "He'll be right out, Father."

Father John tapped his fingers on the counter and fielded the woman's efforts at small talk. How were things at St. Francis? Fine. Fine. Busy as ever, I assume? Oh, yes. Very busy. *Where was the reporter?*

Finally the door next to the counter swung outward and an overweight, round-cheeked man with wire-rimmed glasses and thinning blond hair walked into the lobby. He looked about thirty, despite the paunchy stomach and tell-me-something-new expression in the set of his jaw.

"Hey, Father." The reporter extended a pudgy hand. His grip was moist and nervous. "Didn't expect to see you today. Matter of fact, didn't expect you'd want to talk to me at all. Provincial's office has been stonewalling me on the Father Ryan lawsuit, telling me to talk to the lawyers." He shrugged the massive shoulders. "You know lawyers. Never want to talk to reporters. Come on back."

Father John nodded toward the woman, who was leaning over the counter, eyebrows raised, mouth ajar—*What's going on?*—and followed Todd Hartley into the newsroom past three vacant desks with computers, newspapers, folders, and metal sorting shelves crowding the surfaces. The reporter dragged a chair over to the last desk. "Have a seat," he said. Then he walked around and dropped his bulky frame into a swivel chair and began fumbling through a stack of papers.

"Vicky Holden's sure making a name for herself in Denver," he said.

Father John sat down and hung his cowboy hat on his knee. He didn't say anything. This wasn't about Vicky.

"Handling a real important law case." The reporter pushed on. "*Navajo Nation* v. *Lexcon.* Could impact the interpretations of natural resource law. We've been following it pretty close. Great human interest story, too. Local Indian goes to big city and makes good."

Father John managed a half smile of recognition. He'd been following the story in the *Gazette,* each article conveying the sense that Vicky had disappeared into another space-time continuum, leaving him with an acute sense of loss.

Finally Todd Hartley pulled out a spiral notebook, flipped the top, and jotted something on the blank page. He looked up. Expectancy filled his expression. "Well, Father, what comment do you have on the lawsuit filed against your assistant, Father Don Ryan?"

Father John waited for a couple beats. "I'll give you a statement," he said, "but then I have another story for you."

"Great!" A look that almost passed for glee came into the reporter's face. "So what do you have to say about the lawsuit?"

There was little he could say. Most of what he knew his assistant had told him in confidence. He couldn't repeat it to anyone, let alone a reporter. He said, "It's an unfortunate situation for everybody involved." He was thinking that in two days he would have to give an interview to Don Ryan's lawyers.

The reporter kept his pen poised over the notebook, waiting. "That's it?" He let out a gust of breath. "That's your statement on a one-point-five-million-dollar sexual misconduct suit?"

Father John glanced across the newsroom: the light falling in slats across the crowded desktops, the raincoat dangling from a coattree. He brought his eyes back to the reporter, who was tapping his pen impatiently on the notebook. "Father Don Ryan was at St. Francis three months," he began, selecting the words that he wanted to read in tomorrow's paper. "He's a hardworking, dedicated priest. Very popular with the people, who, I'm sure, are going to miss him."

The reporter scribbled something onto the page. "So he's left the mission?"

"He left today to return to Milwaukee." That was a nonconfidential fact.

The reporter was still writing. "St. Francis is party to the lawsuit, Father. Should judgment go against Father Ryan, how will the mission pay its share of the damages?"

Father John drew in a long breath. He could see the headline: MISSION TO SELL LANDS. The box-store developers would tramp into his office.

"You'll have to ask me that question if and when it happens," he said, struggling to mask the anger still smoldering inside him at what he'd come to think of as Don Ryan's selfishness. Not unlike his own, which made it even more appalling, as if he'd happened past a mirror and unexpectedly caught a true vision of himself.

The reporter shook his head. "Okay, Father O'Malley. I get the picture. You Jesuits are circling the wagons, gathering around to protect one of your own, no matter how guilty the guy might be." He sat back, locking eyes with him for a long moment. Finally he said, "What's the other story about?"

"Duncan Grover."

There was a flicker of recognition in the reporter's eyes. "The suicide?"

"He was murdered."

"You don't say!" The reporter's eyes widened behind his lenses. "Coroner's report says he jumped off a two-hundred-foot cliff at Bear Lake."

Father John waved away the objection. "The coroner's report is wrong. I believe Duncan Grover was thrown off a ledge."

"What makes you think so?"

Father John cleared his throat. Careful, careful, he told himself. He began explaining: Grover had a job waiting at the Arapaho Ranch, he'd been taking instructions from a medicine man, he'd gone to Bear Lake, a holy place, on a vision quest. A man like that didn't kill himself.

Hartley had begun scribbling on another page. After a moment he looked up. "Any evidence somebody tossed him over the cliff?"

Father John was aware of the hum in the fluorescent lights overhead, a pipe knocking somewhere, the splash of traffic outside. He didn't have any evidence. He had a confession that he couldn't use. He said: "There was a warrant out in Colorado for Grover's arrest on robbery charges. He'd been hanging around with some tough characters. He came up here to start over. Somebody could have followed him and killed him. The killer could still be in the area. It could be a man named Eddie."

"What's your source, Father?"

Father John pushed back against his chair. If he gave the reporter Ali Burris's name, the girl would deny she'd ever heard of Eddie. "Let's just say," he began, "I have an anonymous source."

Hartley let the pen drop onto the notebook. "Sorry, Father. I can't print a story based on your anonymous

source. I need names, telephone numbers so I can con-
firm—"

"You rely on anonymous sources all the time, Hartley."
Father John reached across the desk and lifted a folded
newspaper. "How many anonymous sources did you use
in this issue?" He tossed the newspaper aside. "Check out
the warrant in Colorado. Check out the Denver Indian
Center where Grover and Eddie hung out. You're a reporter," he said. "Go after the real story." He was thinking
that a reporter asking questions might convince Slinger to
reopen the investigation.

"I don't know." The reporter rubbed his pudgy hands
together.

"Here's your lead. 'Father John O'Malley, pastor of St.
Francis Mission, has asked Detective Slinger to reopen
the investigation into the death of Duncan Grover.
O'Malley claims that someone by the name of Eddie followed Grover to the reservation from Denver. The man
may have information on Grover's murder.' "

"What's this really about, Father?" The reporter pushed
back in his chair. "What do you care whether some Indian
from Oklahoma committed suicide or got himself murdered?"

"I told you. There could be a killer in the area," he
said. "In Lander. On the res."

"I get it." The reporter shifted his weight forward,
picked up the pen, and began tapping the notebook again.
"The *Gazette* prints this"—he hesitated—"news article,
and the murderer, if the murderer is in the area, starts
worrying about how much you know. He might have to
pay you a little visit. That's it, isn't it? You're trying to
draw Eddie out."

"You know a better way to stop him?"

"Stop him?"

"He killed once. What's to prevent him from killing again?"

"And you could be the next victim." Todd Hartley tossed the pen across the desk and got to his feet. "You're playing a dangerous game, Father."

Father John stood up, facing the man. "You'll run the story?"

"I don't know if my editor's gonna go for it, Father. It's pretty transparent. But I've had a bad feeling about that suicide. Never heard of an Indian killing himself on a vision quest. Something not right about that." He was shaking his head. "I'm trusting that you're giving me a straight story, Father."

"Thanks." Father John shook the other man's hand.

"You might not be thanking me if the killer comes looking for you."

He gave the reporter the most nonchalant wave he could manage and, setting his cowboy hat on his head, made his way back across the newsroom and through the vacant lobby, where a metal curtain had dropped over the counter. He had to turn the key in the door to let himself out.

He drove out of town on 789, veering onto Rendezvous Road, plunging through the late-afternoon shadows that crept over the southern part of the reservation. Every mile or so a house appeared in the open spaces, as if it had erupted from the earth. Todd Hartley was right, he thought. Drawing a killer to himself—to St. Francis Mission—could be dangerous. The article would probably appear in tomorrow's paper, and he was going to have to watch his back.

He turned east on Seventeen Mile Road and, after about

a mile, slowed for a right into the mission grounds. He felt a calm certitude settling over him. One way or another, he and Eddie would cross paths. Let it be before anyone else dies, he prayed.

# ◄ 18 ►

"Adam Elkman's on the line."

Vicky glanced up from the black print on the computer screen, struggling to switch her train of thought from the Navajo Nation brief she was working on. Laola stood in the doorway, an expectant look in the almond-shaped eyes. "You want me to put the call through?"

"Go ahead," Vicky told her, surprised that she'd finally connected with the natural resources director on the reservation. Laola had been trying to reach him since yesterday.

While Vicky waited for her line to ring, she tapped several keys and sent the Navajo Nation brief to the other lawyers on the appeals team. Yesterday Jacob Hazen had called to say that the Navajos wanted to go ahead. The relief and satisfaction in the man's voice had matched her own. Once she had the other lawyers' comments, she'd make the last-minute changes. She intended to deliver her brief to the Tenth Circuit Court tomorrow.

There was a low buzzing sound, and she picked up the receiver. "Adam? How are things on the res?" It was never polite to get right down to business.

"Surprised to get a message from your office yesterday,

Vicky." The man had the low-pitched voice of a TV announcer. "We figured you went off to the big city and forgot all about us."

Vicky swiveled toward the window. Clouds were piling around the tops of nearby skyscrapers. Somewhere a plane was droning. She'd spent four years in Lander waiting for her own people to trust her enough to give her important cases, but the important cases had gone to firms in Casper and Cheyenne. She felt that her people had forgotten her.

The director went on. Lots of rain lately. Roads soggy. Cattle sinking in the mud. She told him about the rainy weather in Denver. Finally she asked if he'd ever heard of diamonds on the reservation.

A guffaw burst through the line. "You gotta be kidding! The Creator put all the diamond deposits down on the Wyoming–Colorado border."

Vicky was quiet a moment, collecting her thoughts. "Is it possible prospectors have been looking for diamonds without the tribe's knowledge?"

There was a long, considered pause. Then: "The res is a big place, Vicky. Lots of remote areas where nobody's around."

She felt a prick of excitement. "So it's possible. Someone could have found a diamond deposit."

"Anything's possible, but you ask me, no prospectors are going to waste time and money looking for diamonds where they've never been found."

Vicky pushed on: "Has any one from Baider Industries contacted you?"

"The diamond mining company?" A note of impatience sounded in the man's voice. "What's this all about, anyway?"

She told him how Vince Lewis, the man in charge of locating new diamond deposits for the company, had contacted her. On the way to meet her he'd been killed. Murdered, she said.

"Never heard of him." Papers crackled at the other end. "Listen, Vicky," the director went on, "I don't think it's a good idea to pursue this. Word gets out that somebody thinks there's diamonds here, it'll be like the gold rush. Hordes of people tramping around the res with shovels and Geiger counters. There aren't any deposits in this part of the state. Talk to Charlie Ferguson in Laramie. He'll tell you the same thing."

"Who?"

"Geology professor at the university. Knows every rock and mineral in the West. Any possibility of diamonds in the geological formations on the res, Ferguson would know about it. Hold on." The line went dead for a couple seconds. Then the director's voice again: "Here's his number."

Vicky scribbled down the number, thanked the director, and hung up. She stared at the phone. Either Adam Elkman didn't know about any deposits, or he was lying, maybe taking a kickback himself from Baider Industries to keep a deposit secret. She didn't think so. Elkman had been the natural resources director for three years; the people trusted him. And he'd sounded genuinely surprised when she'd mentioned diamonds.

And yet . . . There were miles of open plains on the reservation where men and trucks could dissolve like flecks of dust in the atmosphere. A small crew could prospect for diamonds without anyone knowing, except the owner of Baider Industries. And Vince Lewis, who died before he could blow the whistle.

*If* there were diamonds on the reservation. She was chasing a phantom. She had no proof of the existence of diamond deposits within two hundred miles of the reservation.

She picked up the phone again and dialed the number Elkman had given her. After a woman answered—"Geology department"—she was connected to an answering machine. "This is Professor Ferguson. Please leave a message." She told him who she was, asked if she could see him tomorrow, and left her number.

From the corridor came the sounds of a printer whirring, the subdued voices of people passing by. A phone rang in a nearby office. The intense busyness of Howard and Fergus.

She stared at her own phone, wondering again what Vince Lewis's wife might know about his work. Vicky could still see the auburn-haired woman weaving down the brightly lit corridor toward her dying husband. A little chill ran through her. If Jana Lewis had any idea of why her husband had been killed, her life could also be in danger.

Vicky pressed the intercom button and asked Laola to get the address for Vince Lewis's wife.

Within a couple minutes Laola was in her office again, flapping some sheets of paper. "Phone book lists V and J Lewis on Vine Street." She laid one sheet on the desk. "And the answering service took a message yesterday from Father John." The second sheet dropped on the first. "He's looking for a Pueblo Indian named Eddie. Hangs around the Indian Center. Thinks the Indian might know something about the suicide at Bear Lake."

Vicky took the second sheet and scanned the message. *Please call me.* She hadn't talked to John O'Malley since she'd moved back to Denver. There had been no legitimate reason, no excuse, to call him. Now the suicide at Bear Lake. And John O'Malley, looking for the truth about what had happened there. He understood. No warrior would kill himself in a sacred place, on a vision quest. She felt a stab of guilt that she wasn't there to help.

"You heard about the lawsuit?" Laola said.

"What lawsuit?" Vicky picked up the phone and started tapping out the number at St. Francis Mission.

Laola leaned over the desk. "Moccasin telegraph," she began in a confidential tone, "says some woman's filed a one-and-a-half-million-dollar sexual misconduct suit against the priest at St. Francis."

Vicky dropped the receiver into the cradle. Assistant priests came and went, but for almost eight years, John O'Malley had been *the* priest at St. Francis. She could imagine some woman falling in love with him. She could imagine *that.* But he was a priest; he kept his vows. She knew him—she had thought she knew him. Was it possible she'd been wrong? That she didn't know him at all? How could that be? A kind of numbness was spreading through her.

She realized dimly that Laola was staring at her, watching for her reaction. She needed some time to reconcile her own sense of John O'Malley with this new image. "See if you can get Mrs. Lewis for me," Vicky said, making an effort to keep her voice steady. No matter what may have happened, he was trying to find the truth about Duncan Grover's death. She decided to drop by the Indian Center after work and see if anyone knew a Pueblo Indian named Eddie.

The secretary turned and walked out of the office. In half a minute the phone buzzed, and Vicky lifted the receiver. There was a click, followed by the electronic hum of another answering machine and a woman's voice: "We aren't here, but please leave a message. We really want to talk to you. Have a great day."

Vicky hung up. She wondered how Jana Lewis spent her days. Banging on Steve Clark's door demanding that he solve her husband's murder? Huddling with a lawyer about her husband's estate?

She would drop by the house on Vine Street later, before she went to the Indian Center. If Jana Lewis was in, she would ask to speak with her a moment. It was always better to catch a witness off guard.

As soon as she made the decision, she felt better, calmer. What did it matter if John O'Malley had dropped his guard and gotten involved with some woman? He was human. People made mistakes. She had made her share. What difference would it make to her if he'd made a mistake? She had her own work, her own life. She intended to find out what Vince Lewis's wife knew. And she had something for Jana Lewis: a warning that the woman could be in danger.

# ◆ 19 ◆

Vicky pointed the Bronco through the traffic spilling out of downtown Denver and turned left onto Speer Boulevard. The sun blinked in the rearview mirror, but black rain clouds were gathering over the mountains. Traffic was heavy, four lanes across, winding southeast along the banks of Cherry Creek. Ten minutes later the grounds of the Denver Country Club came into view outside her passenger window, the sprawling, gray-frame building a mute symbol of another century, built by the people who had displaced her own.

Another left turn down a wide street. Rows of mansions passing outside. She parked in front of a redbrick Tudor separated from the street by a sweep of glistening wet lawn and bushes that dipped under cascades of yellow and pink buds. Fallen buds crunched under her heels as she walked up the sidewalk. She clapped the brass door knocker.

There was no sound coming from the house, yet she had the sense that someone was there. She rapped again, giving the knocker a hard kick this time. Still no answer. She glanced at her watch—five twenty-six—and debated whether to wait or drive over to the Indian Center, see if anyone there had ever heard of Eddie, then drive back.

The thought of driving across the city all evening filled her with dread. She knocked again.

The door inched open. The auburn-haired woman from the emergency room peered through the crack. Slim, red-tipped fingers wrapped around the door's edge. On the third finger was a wide gold band with a diamond the size of a marble floating in the center. "What is it?"

Vicky told the woman her name and said she'd like to talk to her a moment.

The crack widened, and the woman leaned unsteadily forward, still gripping the door. Her face was pale—no makeup, a puffiness around the eyes, which had the surreal color of green glass. She was in a blue terrycloth robe that bunched around her waist. Her dark, shoulder-length hair looked tangled and uncombed, as if she'd just lifted her head from a pillow. "I saw you at the hospital," she said in a resigned monotone.

"Yes, I was there."

"One of Vince's whores."

"What?"

"How dare you come here? You have no right—" The door started to close.

"I'm an attorney, Mrs. Lewis." Vicky placed a hand against the door. "Your husband called me the morning of his death. I was on my way to meet him for the first time when he was killed. I'd like to talk to you."

Jana Lewis blinked. A new wariness came into the green eyes. For the first time Vicky caught the syrupy odor of some kind of liqueur. The woman was slightly drunk. Finally the door swung open into a spacious entryway with shadows falling over the white and black floor tiles and running up the wide staircase. The woman tottered through an archway on the right, each step deliberate and focused. There was the sound of a clock chiming somewhere.

Vicky hesitated, then stepped inside and followed the woman into a large drawing room with gray sofas and chairs against the paneled walls and a marble fireplace across from the entry. Oil paintings in carved wooden frames hung in perfect symmetry around the walls. The brass lamp on a side table threw a dim circle of light over an Oriental carpet.

Jana Lewis positioned herself in front of the fireplace, one hand braced against the mantel for support. The other held a crystal goblet half-full of golden-brown liquid that shimmered in the light.

"I get it now," she said, comprehension moving behind her eyes. "You're the divorce lawyer." She spit out the words, and tiny flecks of moisture dotted the goblet. "Well, here I am, the wife you were going to dig up a lot of dirt on so that bastard could get my money." She raised the goblet and took a long drink. "I'm almost sorry we'll miss our little day in court. Ah, the justice to see Vince get what was coming to him, which was nothing. I would have taken him for everything he had. I would have ruined him. The company lawyers were on my side, you know. The damned best in the state." A half smile of satisfaction came into the green eyes.

Vicky said, "I'm not here about your divorce. Your husband arranged the meeting to discuss another matter."

The woman raised her eyes over the rim of the goblet. "Another matter? What could it possibly have to do with me?" She bent over a small table, lifted a rounded bottle, and shakily refilled the goblet, then dropped into a chair. "I'm sure you don't want a drink. You being Indian."

Vicky felt the sting, like a pellet spit into her face by a passing semi. What did the woman think? That every

Indian was either a falling-down drunk or in recovery? She swallowed back the impulse to set her straight. "Your husband—"

"Don't call him that."

"I assumed you were married."

"Legally. I haven't thought of the bastard, when I thought of him at all, as my husband for a very long time. We hadn't spoken in months."

"This must be hard on you," Vicky heard herself saying. She was beginning to regret having come here. If the woman hadn't spoken to her husband in months, it was unlikely she knew what he'd been working on.

"Not really." Jana Lewis's voice lifted with a false bravado. "I've made a life without him. All I needed was the legal paper setting me free. Naturally I thought it would be a divorce decree, not a death certificate. But either way . . ." She raised the goblet in a mock toast and took another drink.

"Forgive me," Vicky said. "I shouldn't have bothered you."

"Then why did you? Why did you come here? What do you want of me?" Jana Lewis set the goblet on the table. The brown liquid sloshed over her hand.

Vicky walked over and perched on a chair. "I was hoping you could tell me what your husband"—she hesitated—"what Vince wanted to talk to me about the day he died. Did he ever mention a diamond deposit on the Wind River Reservation?"

A flicker—no more—came into the other woman's eyes, and then it was gone. "Diamonds on an Indian reservation?" She let out a sharp laugh and leaned toward the table to refill the goblet. "Vince would go to the moon if he thought there were diamonds there," she said, "but I can assure you he never went to a reservation."

Even as the woman spoke, Vicky knew it wasn't true. Something in the tone—the nonchalance, the note of dismissal—sounded forced and out of place. "You said you hadn't spoken to Vince in three months," she said, slipping into her courtroom tone, as if Jana Lewis were on the witness stand. "How do you know he wasn't on the reservation recently?"

"Because I know his every move." Jana Lewis waved the goblet. "Every restaurant and bar and whore's house. My private investigator will tell you he didn't go to any reservation."

"Private investigator?" This was more than Vicky had hoped for—a PI following Vince Lewis, noting exactly whom he'd seen, whom he'd talked to. "You told Detective Clark?"

"And why would I do that? I called off the private investigator when I had enough to file the divorce. Besides it's not police business. The last thing I need is for the newspapers to hear about it." She threw back her head and gave another forced laugh. "Oh, I can see the headlines. 'Denver Socialite Hired PI to Watch Bastard Husband.' " Shifting sideways a little, she took another drink. "Daddy's upset enough over the publicity about Vince's death. Not exactly a respectable way to go—run down like a dog. Daddy would have much preferred a more appropriate hunting accident. But, I say, what the hell, he's gone."

Vicky leaned toward her. "Mrs. Lewis," she said, "I believe your husband was murdered."

The woman's head snapped around, as if she'd caught an unexpected blow. The liqueur dribbled over her fingers. She was staring wide-eyed, a fixed expression of disbelief and outrage in the pale face. "That's ridiculous! Vince's death was an accident."

She looked away and started to get up—a shaky commandeering of the floor. She gripped a corner of the table to steady herself. The goblet tipped sideways, spilling liqueur down the front of the blue robe. "Please go," she said.

Vicky got to her feet and faced the woman. "Mrs. Lewis, if your husband had located a diamond deposit on the reservation, for your own safety, please tell me."

Jana Lewis gave a shout of laughter. "My safety? Don't be ridiculous."

"If you don't want to talk to me," Vicky went on, "then talk to Detective Clark."

"Detective Clark"—an expulsion of breath—"is looking for the drunk that ran Vince down. If he's wasting time chasing some crazy murder theory, my father will see that he's removed from the investigation. We are not without influence in this town, Ms. Holden. Daddy'll have Detective Clark's job." She pushed away from the table, reclaiming her footing. "Get out," she said.

Vicky got to her feet and started for the door. She turned back. "Be careful," she said. "Your husband was murdered, and your life may also be in danger." She left Jana Lewis pouring another drink.


The Bronco's engine burst into life at the turn of the ignition. It had started to rain—a light misting that sparkled like diamonds in the headlights and pecked at the windshield as Vicky turned west onto Speer and worked her way into the fastest lane, making the lights as yellow switched to red, wondering if a wealthy woman with a powerful father would hire someone to kill her husband, even for a three-million-dollar insurance policy. It was possible. Except that Jana Lewis had seemed shocked at the mention of murder.

And yet, the woman knew more than she'd admitted, Vicky was sure. Another picture was starting to emerge, like an image gradually taking shape in a developing tray: Nathan Baider following Jana Lewis down the hospital corridor.

Nathan Baider and Jana Lewis.

It would explain why the company's law firm would represent Jana in the divorce. Why Vince Lewis had wanted to dig up dirt on a wife who intended to ruin him. It could even explain why Lewis had wanted to blow the whistle on Baider Industries.

Vicky dug her cell phone out of her bag on the seat beside her and, at the next red light, tapped out Steve Clark's number. His answering service picked up. She said she had a hunch that Jana Lewis knew why her husband had been killed. "Call me as soon as you can," she said.

In the distance, the shadows of the mountains merged into the rain-filled sky. She glanced at the dashboard clock. Almost six-fifteen. Marie Champlain would be in her office at the Indian Center, supervising the evening classes and meetings.

She made a right, circled beneath the Speer Viaduct and merged with the southbound traffic on I-25. A sheet of water billowed over her windshield from the tires of the semi ahead. She changed lanes and sped past.

# ‹ 20 ›

Vicky parked in the graveled lot of the tan brick elementary school that was now the Denver Indian Center. This was the Indian neighborhood: white bungalows with pickups in the driveways and sofas and chairs crammed onto the porches. Rain danced in the streetlights.

Inside, the building retained the feel of a school, with bright fluorescent lights illuminating the notices tacked along the walls. Doors on either side led to classrooms that now served as offices and meeting halls. Through the glass in the doors, Vicky could see Indian people seated around tables: dark skin and black hair, like punctuation marks against the whitewashed walls.

She knocked at the door with the black-lettered sign below the glass: DIRECTOR. A pickup basketball game was going on in the gym at the far end of the corridor. The grunts and shouts mingled with the thud of a dribbled basketball. From behind the office door, silence.

She was about to retrace her steps when Marie Champlain came through another door. A stocky woman, not more than five feet tall, with the black hair and pinkish skin of a breed. She wore a loose-fitting blue dress that flapped around her thick legs.

"Vicky? Was I expecting you?" She hurried forward, as if she were late for some forgotten appointment.

Vicky shook her head. "Do you have a minute?"

"For our own Indian lawyer, always." The woman brushed past and opened the office door.

Vicky followed her into a small space with a desk and a two-seat black vinyl couch pushed against one wall. Papers and folders spilled over the desk and trailed across the couch in haphazard stacks. The director swooped up a handful of papers from the couch. "No sense standing when we can sit, I always say." She settled into the chair at the desk and tossed the papers onto a sloping pile.

"How've you been?" Vicky began.

"Oh, holdin' up okay." The other woman entered into the familiar pattern. Gloomy days. Not much sunshine. "Our people been living in the sun so long we start feeling depressed when it goes away." She glanced about, as if another idea had taken hold. "We got more and more Indian people here every day lookin' for help. Sick, out of work, don't have any place to leave the kids. Don't have anything, some of 'em. No household stuff, no food. We try to get them fixed up with social services till they get on their feet."

Vicky nodded. She'd heard the stories many times, and with them came the pain of unwanted memories. She, in a car with a hundred thousand miles on the odometer and a reverse gear that didn't always work, driving to Denver to begin a new life, an old suitcase and a couple of boxes in the backseat holding everything she owned, the city sprawling ahead, stark and impersonal.

She drew in a long breath and shifted toward the edge of the couch, the preliminaries now over. "I'm looking for a Pueblo Indian named Eddie. He hung around with Duncan Grover."

The director's face froze. "That was one troublemaker, Grover," she said. "Came around for a couple of pow-wows. You could smell the whiskey when he walked in the door. Beat up some Indian out in the parking lot about a month ago. Couple guys broke it up before I had to call the police." She shrugged. "We'd just as soon not have the police coming out here too often. They get to think Indians are nothing but troublemakers. Anyway—" Another shrug. "Next thing I hear on the moccasin telegraph Grover's jumped off a ledge at Bear Lake."

The director let her eyes trail toward the corridor beyond the opened door. "Couldn't believe my ears. Grover might've been a troublemaker, but I never heard of a warrior taking a flying leap off a ledge in a sacred place. Don't make sense."

Vicky nodded. It hadn't made sense to her either, or to John O'Malley.

She said, "Father O'Malley thinks Eddie might know something about the death."

"Never met the good priest." The director broke into a smile. "Heard lots about him. People from the res say he's a white man they can trust."

True, Vicky thought. She had always trusted him, but now—the lawsuit . . . She went on: "If Grover was a troublemaker, somebody might have had a grudge against him."

The director sat back and regarded her a moment. "Lots of people, you ask me."

"What about the guy he got into a fight with?"

"Yeah, him for sure. He was a bloody mess, but soon's the other guys pulled Grover off, he got himself into a brown pickup and tore outta here."

"Who was he?" Vicky tried to keep the urgency out of her voice.

"Never saw him before that night." The woman gave a halfhearted shrug. "Never seen him since. I can't say I'm sorry about that."

"Is there anyone else who knew Grover? Anyone who might know who Eddie is?"

"Sorry." Marie shook her head, then stared straight ahead a moment, as if she were contemplating an image on the wall. "You say Eddie is Pueblo. I can ask around, get back to you."

"Thanks, Marie." Vicky stood up and started for the door. She had the same feeling that had come over her earlier, after talking with Jana Lewis: she was chasing phantoms. Rumors and shadows, like evil spirits, always ahead, around a corner, out of sight, laughing at her.

"Hold on a minute." Marie was on her feet, shouldering past into the corridor. The clack of her footsteps mingled with the *thump, thump* of a basketball. After a moment she was back, a tall, well-built Indian behind her. He looked about thirty, with the dark, round face and intent look of the Cheyenne and black hair smoothed back into a ponytail. He bunched his fists in the pockets of his blue jeans jacket.

"This here's Robert Yellow Wolf." Marie tilted her head back. "He was one of the guys broke up the fight in the parking lot." She glanced up and gave him an appreciative smile.

"Did you know Grover?" Vicky asked.

"Nah." Yellow Wolf shook his head slowly. "That dude give Indians a bad name. Didn't surprise me none he jumped off a cliff."

"What about somebody called Eddie?"

He was still shaking his head. "Never had the pleasure. But he could've been the guy Grover beat hell out of. I

heard him shouting something like, 'Eddie, you sonovabitch, I'm gonna kill ya.' "

So he did exist, Vicky thought. Eddie was real. Not an
untrue image. Real, and possibly a murderer.

"Eddie who?" Vicky persisted.

"Eddie sonovabitch." The Indian shrugged.

Vicky drove north on Sheridan Boulevard through neigh-
borhoods of white frame bungalows, brick ranches, and
strip malls anchored by gas stations and fast-food restaurants. The rain had stopped, leaving the air heavy with
the smell of wet leaves and grasses. The evening traffic
was light: arrows of yellow headlights blurring over the
asphalt, the sound of tires splashing through puddles in
the intersections.

She would call John O'Malley the minute she got
home, she decided. She was ready now. The lawsuit had
been in the back of her mind all day. She'd felt betrayed
somehow. It was silly. Whatever had happened—it had
nothing to do with her.

He would be in the residence now—she could picture
him—in the study, as crammed with papers and books as
her own, the music from some opera blasting around him.
She'd tell him what she'd learned. Eddie had reason to
hold a grudge against Duncan Grover. And the promise
Marie had made to keep asking around on the chance
someone might know the man.

She wondered what difference it would make if John
O'Malley did find Eddie. It was all theory and shadows.
Visions of what had happened. There was no physical
evidence, or the coroner would have ruled the death a
homicide and the police would be looking for Eddie.

She turned right onto Twenty-ninth Avenue. Downtown

lights rose in the distance. After a few blocks, she made a U-turn and parked behind another vehicle in front of the white house rising from the bluff. "Spirits dwell on the bluffs," her grandmother had said.

For a brief moment a sense of loneliness and disorientation hit her, and along with it, a dread of going into the house, wrapped in the quiet of its thick walls. Lucas was out to dinner with his new boss; he'd been out almost every evening since he'd arrived. He planned to move into his own apartment in a few days. She would be alone again. *Hisei ci nihi.* Woman alone. The grandmothers had given her an appropriate name, she thought.

She started up the concrete steps, trying to shake off the odd feeling. The house loomed above, shadows falling off the steeply pitched roof and clinging to the oblong windows and the stucco. The gate at the top of the stairs squealed when she opened it. She closed it behind her, then stopped.

Something wasn't right, some slight disturbance in the atmosphere. An animal, she told herself, aware of the prickly feeling on her skin. She remained motionless, her eyes searching the shadows on the front porch until she saw the figure of a man rising from the bench inside the railing. He started down the sidewalk toward her.

She clasped her keys tightly, the jagged metal cutting into her fingers. "Who's there?" she called, moving back toward the gate, her other hand brushing the air, searching for the latch. She heard her own voice again, disembodied somewhere ahead of her. "What do you want?"

# ‹ 21 ›

"Vicky, it's me. Steve."

She held on to the latch a moment and made herself breathe slowly—in and out, in and out. In the dim light of a passing car, she could see the familiar slouch of his shoulders, the easy angle of his posture as he walked down the sidewalk. Hands in his slacks pockets, the fronts of the dark sport coat pushed back, tie loosened at the collar of a light shirt.

"Sorry, Vicky," he said. "I didn't mean to frighten you. I got your call, and since I was in the neighborhood . . ." He hesitated, and she knew it wasn't true. "I took a chance on finding you home. Been sitting on the porch waiting. I just decided to give you another ten minutes, and here you are."

"Let's go inside," Vicky managed, not trusting herself to say more. Her throat felt as scratchy as sagebrush, as if she'd been riding all day on the plains. She moved past him, aware of his footsteps, soft and measured, behind her. She jabbed the key at the lock, her hand shaking.

"Let me," Steve said. The shadow of his arm reached around her, and his hand covered her own. "I'm good at this sort of thing." In a half second the door swung open. She stepped inside and flipped on the wall switch, sending a flood of light over the entry, the living room on the left. She made her way through the shadows of the dining room ahead, dropping her bag on the table, and into the kitchen. Another wall switch. The fluorescent ceiling light stuttered into life as she opened the refrigerator and removed a bottle of water.

"Something to drink?" she asked. "Some coffee?" She turned back to the man leaning against the doorjamb, relaxed and watchful, hands still in his pockets.

"Water's fine for me." He nodded at the bottle in her hand.

Vicky found two glasses in the cupboard and filled them almost to the brim. She handed him one, then began gulping the water in the other glass, not stopping until it was empty. She refilled the glass, feeling calmer now, in control again.

"You seem pretty jumpy." He was still watching her. "What's going on?"

Vicky leaned back against the counter and locked eyes with the man. "You scared me, Steve. I wasn't expecting anyone to be on my porch."

"That's it?"

Not all of it, she thought. It was the city, the jumble of noises and odors, the unnatural play of light and shadows around the buildings, and the odd feeling that some stranger, not herself, floated over the paved streets that glistened with wetness, past the houses and buildings that crowded the earth, while she—her own spirit—was on the reservation.

She nodded, ignoring the perplexity in his expression. She could never explain.

"How about we go get something to eat?" he said after a moment, the perplexity giving way to something that resembled hope.

It was the hunger bothering her, that was all. She agreed.

"I know just the place," Steve said, relief in his tone, as if this were the easiest problem he'd faced all day. "Little restaurant couple blocks away." He set his half-full glass on the counter. "You'd better follow me. I'm backup for another guy tonight."

Vicky followed the white Ford through the streets of north Denver. Bungalows and Victorians slid by outside, light glowing in the windows. The remnants of the earlier rain still shone on the asphalt. She turned onto Thirty-second Avenue and parked behind the Ford in front of a row of little shops and restaurants. Cars lumbered past, tires thrumming into the background of city noise.

He took her arm and guided her inside, through a maze of tables with checkered cloths and candles blinking in the center. Only a few other diners were there.

"So you're finally having dinner with me," he said after they'd sat down.

"Just business, Steve." She gave him a friendly smile and began studying the menu, a part of her wondering what it might have been like, how her life might have gone, had she ever felt something more than friendship for this man.

After the waitress had taken their orders, he said, "Tell me about your hunch, Vicky."

It was a moment before she realized he was referring to the call she'd placed to him earlier. She sat back, folding and refolding the white cloth napkin in her lap, and explained that she'd gone to see Jana Lewis.

"Now, why would you do that?" He made no effort to conceal his irritation. "I told you I'd get back to you the minute we had anything on Vince Lewis's death. Why can't you trust me to do my job, Vicky?"

She waited until the waitress had delivered plates of chicken dumplings and poured two mugs of coffee. "Of course I trust you, Steve," she said.

"I don't think so."

In his eyes, Vicky caught an image of the woman he was staring at: determined, stubborn. She was as transparent as the windowpane next to their table. "I have to know what Vince Lewis wanted to tell me," she said.

He seemed to consider this, cutting into the chicken, taking a bite. Finally he said, "I want to get to the bottom of Lewis's death as much as you do. I want to find the son of a bitch who was driving that car, and put him away for the rest of his miserable life. Problem is, you talking to Jana Lewis could jeopardize the investigation. Right now the grieving widow could be the number-one suspect."

"I don't think Jana Lewis had anything to do with her husband's murder."

Steve stabbed at another piece of chicken. "Mind telling me what brought you to this conclusion?"

"She had no idea her husband was murdered," Vicky said. "She was convinced his death was an accident."

The detective took another bite and began chewing slowly, his eyes not leaving hers. "You realize," he said finally, "that you'll have to testify about your conversation if we put Jana Lewis on trial for murder. Hiring somebody to kill her husband is the same as doing the deed herself."

"There's no motivation, Steve." Vicky felt herself moving onto firmer ground. It was the feeling she had in the courtroom when she knew a case was won.

"Oh, no? Three million dollars isn't enough motivation for you?"

"Jana comes from a wealthy, influential family," Vicky plunged on. "The mansion is probably hers. Why would she take a chance on throwing it all away?"

Steve shrugged. "You ever know wealthy people with enough money? There's never enough, Vicky."

"Jana had started divorce proceedings," she said.

"I know that." He looked away, and she could see the vein pulsing in his neck.

"The point is," she went on, "Jana Lewis was represented by the company's lawyers." She had his attention now. "Vince was the vice-president, not his wife. Why didn't the lawyers represent him?"

"You're the lawyer," Steve said, a harshness in his tone that surprised her. He might have been interrogating a street thug. "Suppose you tell me?"

She drew in a long breath. "I think Jana Lewis is having an affair with Nathan Baider. He arranged for a divorce attorney at the company's firm to represent her."

"Jesus, Vicky. First it's diamonds on the reservation. Now Jana Lewis and Nathan Baider are having an affair. Where's the evidence? Nobody's ever heard of diamonds up there, and nobody at Baider Industries has mentioned Jana and the boss in the same breath." He leaned toward her, his voice low now, precisely controlled. "I want you out of this investigation, understand? Your theories stink. Forget about Vince Lewis."

Vicky dropped her napkin beside her plate. "Sometimes, Steve, you can be a real bastard." She got to her feet, took her bag from the back of the chair, and started for the door. What he'd said had the sting of truth. She had a theory. There was no evidence. She was forcing every scrap of information into her own preconceived image of what had happened. Why should it matter to her that some white man killed another white man?

She was across the sidewalk and walking around the Bronco when Steve caught up with her, took her arm, and turned her toward him. His grip was strong. She tried to pull away, scraping the back of her leg on the bumper.

"You're right," he said. "I'm a bastard. But I can't stand the idea of your being involved in murder. If there's anything to your theory—I'm not saying there is—then it could be dangerous. Whoever wanted Lewis dead could want you dead, too. I can't stand to think about it, Vicky."

"It's okay," she said, finally pulling free.

He took her hand. "Please try to understand. It's just that I feel so damn helpless, so frustrated, every time I see you. Every time I think of you, and . . ." He paused. "I mean, couldn't you like me a little?"

"You know I like you, Steve," she said, forgiving him, an old friend from that time when she was scared and alone, except for the young white man fresh out of the navy.

"I'm asking for something more, Vicky." He tightened his hand around hers. "I can be a bastard, but I'm working on that."

She slipped her hand free and ran a finger along the edge of his jaw. She could feel the prickly growth of today's beard. "I'm sorry," she said. "You're a good man. You deserve more."

A phone started ringing, a muffled noise nearly lost in the dark evening. He reached inside his sport coat and extracted a small black cell phone. "Clark," he said, his eyes on hers, as if he could hold her in place.

A second passed, then another. His lips moved close to the phone. "I'll be right there." He tapped a button and slipped the phone back inside his coat.

"What is it?" she said. Please, God, she was thinking. Not another murder.

"Vicky . . ." He hesitated. "I'm sorry, Vicky. A patrol car just spotted a woman's body dumped next to the tracks behind the Union Station. It's Jana Lewis."

"What?" Vicky felt the muscles in her stomach constrict, and her throat went dry.

"Looks like somebody beat her to death." Steve took her hand again, then let it go. "I'll call you," he said.

He whirled around and ran to the Ford. A second passed, and the car turned into the street and accelerated, leaving behind the faintest smell of exhaust.

Vicky retraced her route through the neighborhood. Left turn. Down three blocks. Another left. Only half-aware of the houses lining the streets, as if some part of her had switched into automatic. She parked the Bronco in front of her house, went inside, and dropped onto a dining-room chair next to the phone. She dialed the number at St. Francis Mission.

# ◆ 22 ◆

"Father O'Malley." He had picked up the phone on the first ring.

Even before she spoke, he knew Vicky was on the other end. The months collapsed into the moment. It was as if she had never left. He waited. The sounds of "O! mio babbino caro" drifted around him. Beyond the study, the residence was encased in quiet. Light from the lamps on Circle Drive glowed in the window and mingled with the circle of light over his desk.

Finally the words burst through the line in a sob. "I have to talk to you, John."

"What's happened? Are you okay?" He reached around and turned down the volume on the tape player. Then he pressed the receiver against his ear, listening for the sounds of her breath. "Vicky, are you okay?" he asked again.

"A woman I met today was just murdered." She blurted out the words.

"Tell me about it."

He heard her take in a long breath. Then the shuddering explanation. First, a man by the name of Vince Lewis, on the way to meet her, run down by a car. And this evening, his wife, Jana, beaten to death near the railroad tracks.

She'd gone to see the woman earlier, mentioned that her husband had been murdered. The woman was drunk, shocked at the idea of murder.

"My God, John. What if she confronted the killer about her husband's murder? I could be responsible for her death."

"Listen to me, Vicky," he said, switching to his counseling voice, firm and steady. "The woman was drunk. She could have gone to a bar and picked up somebody. There's no telling what a drunk might do. Drunks aren't rational." That was true. He had been at his irrational best when he was drunk.

She'd drawn in a ragged breath and told him that Vince Lewis had worked for a diamond mining company, Baider Industries. "I think he might have found a diamond deposit on the reservation. The company is hiding it."

It surprised him. He'd never heard of diamond mines here.

"A crew could be working in a remote area." Her voice gained urgency. "They could be removing gems right under the noses of the tribes and not paying royalties. And they may never have to pay royalties if the appeals court doesn't reverse—" She paused. "In any case, Jana Lewis denied knowing anything, but I think she was covering for the company's founder, Nathan Baider. I think they were having an affair. He might have killed her."

"You don't know that, Vicky."

The sobbing started again, a muffled sound, as if she'd placed a palm over the mouthpiece. "So many people dead because of me," she managed.

He didn't say anything for a moment. She'd shot a man last year to save his life. It was a heavy burden, and he wished he could take it from her, that she didn't have to carry it alone.

"Is Lucas there?" he said finally.

The line was silent for a couple seconds. Then she told him that Lucas had started a new job, that he'd probably move into an apartment soon. "He doesn't need my problems," she said.

"He's your son, Vicky. He loves you."

"I have to be strong for the kids, John. They have to see me strong."

"You don't have to be strong for everybody." He knew that she believed otherwise. Everybody saw her strength. Only a few saw her vulnerability. Ben Holden, he knew. And himself. This new thought made him feel absurdly close to her.

"I can't let them get away with it," she said.

He understood who she was talking about. "Baider Industries is a company, Vicky. They're bound to have a lot of power. Let the police handle this. It's not your responsibility."

"Vince Lewis was on his way to see *me*. His wife may have died because of *me*. Don't tell me I have no responsibility."

"Then forgive yourself," he said. "You didn't intend any harm. You had nothing to do with their deaths."

"You know, John O'Malley, sometimes you can be too damn logical." He could picture the red flush that came into her cheeks when she was angry. "All your beautiful logic can get in the way of the truth."

Perhaps, he thought.

"I guess I needed the logic anyway," she said, her voice calmer now. The line went quiet for a couple seconds. "I got your message," she said finally. Then she told him what she'd learned about Eddie: he wasn't a regular at the Indian Center, but he'd been there about a month ago. He drove a brown pickup. Grover had beaten him up in

the parking lot. "Maybe he followed Grover to the reservation and killed him," she said.

He smiled. It wasn't the first time they'd reached the
same conclusion.

"How did you know about Eddie?" she asked.

He'd gotten the name from Grover's girlfriend, he told
her. An Indian girl, working in a convenience store, too
scared to talk to the police.

"She can tie Eddie to Grover." The urgency had returned. "Eddie could come after her, too. She could be in
danger, John."

Another conclusion they shared, he thought. He said,
"If I can flush him out—"

"How are you going to do that?"

He stopped himself from telling her about the newspaper article. "Let's just say I'm trying to locate him. If
I get his name, Detective Slinger will pick him up for
questioning."

She was quiet, and he had the sense something else was
on her mind. After a moment she said, "What about the
lawsuit?"

He didn't want to talk about the lawsuit. Just thinking
about it filled him with a mixture of anger and shame.
"My new assistant, Don Ryan—"

"Assistant!" she interrupted.

He felt as if he'd taken a fastball in his chest. Had she
thought he was the target of the lawsuit? My God, what
did she think of him?

"It was an affair, Vicky," he said finally, keeping his
voice steady. "He'd been counseling her. If the case goes
to court, the woman will probably win. The provincial
doesn't believe insurance will cover all the damages."

"Where does that leave the mission?"

"We'll have to sell the land along the highway," he

heard himself saying. He felt as if he were talking about selling a part of himself. "There probably wouldn't have been enough money to build the day-care and a new senior center, anyway."

"Oh, John. You had such hopes . . ." She let the thought trail away. "I'm sorry," she said.

So was he, he thought. "Listen, Vicky," he went on, "promise me you'll be careful. Don't put yourself in any danger."

"Same to you, John O'Malley," she said.

Father John watched the ball arc high over center field. "Move in!" he yelled, cupping one hand over his mouth like a megaphone. The sound of his voice floated through the afternoon air, still damp from yesterday's rain. But the sky was as crystalline blue as a mountain lake, and the sun was warm on his back. He'd called Eldon Antelope this morning to announce a practice, and this afternoon fifteen kids had shown up.

Now Randy White Horse was sprinting across the field, the small, intent brown face turned into the sun. He reached up and grabbed the ball out of the air, making it look easy.

"All right!" Father John shook his fist. He'd been pacing the field for almost two hours, drilling the kids on fly balls, grounders—whatever came their way. The field looked as if it had been plowed, with ridges of mud erupting through the barely dried surface.

"Weight back, eye on the ball!" Eldon Antelope shouted to the hitter. His son, Joseph, was on first base, jamming a fist into his glove.

So far the Eagles looked good, the way they were hitting the ball, shagging the flies, scooping up the grounders. Almost as if they'd played the last game yesterday instead of six months ago. Barring any unforeseen catastrophes—injuries or dropouts—they had a good chance of winning the league title. For a moment Father John felt like a kid again on the sandlots in Boston. The world could be crazy, an out-of-whack place, but everything was right on the diamond.

This would be a great season, he told himself, trying to ignore the uneasiness that had nagged at him since Vicky's call last night. "Let her be safe," he prayed silently, his eyes on the ball shooting past the pitcher's mound out into center field. Randy was skidding sideways, and then he had it. His face stretched into a wide grin.

Father John gave him a thumbs-up. Out of the corner of his eye he saw the bulky figure of Matt Slinger walking down the third-base line: the rumpled slacks and open sport coat, the dark tie skewed sideways over the white shirt. The man's shoulders curved forward in determination.

He'd been half expecting the detective since he'd read the headline in this morning's *Gazette*: PRIEST DISPUTES SUICIDE. He flashed a signal to Eldon behind the plate that he needed a few minutes, then walked toward the detective.

"Hope this is important," he said, closing the distance between them. "We've got a practice going on."

Slinger planted his boots a couple of feet apart in the soft earth. His hands hung at his sides like baseball gloves. In one glove hand was a rolled-up copy of the newspaper. "You got some information about Duncan Grover's death, you come to me, Father O'Malley, not some newspaper reporter." He waved the newspaper between them like a baton.

"I told you I don't believe Grover committed suicide."

"Yeah? How come you didn't tell me about your so-called source?" The man stepped closer. Little specks of perspiration blossomed on his forehead. "I need names, O'Malley."

Father John was quiet a moment. He had two sources: the man in the confessional and a scared Indian girl who would probably deny everything she'd told him. And now he had Vicky.

"Check the Denver Indian Center, Detective," he said. "Last month Grover beat up a Pueblo Indian named Eddie. I think Eddie's still around."

"You think—"

Father John put up one hand. "Trust me, Slinger. He drives a brown pickup with out-of-state license plates. Bring him in. See if he has an alibi for the day Grover was killed."

The detective took a couple steps backward. His jaw moved silently a moment before he said, "I'm onto you, Father O'Malley. You conned the *Gazette* into running this bullshit that makes the department look bad, like we brushed off the death of an Indian. Well, you outsmarted yourself. If you're right, Grover's killer might decide you know too much. He could show up here. What're you gonna do? I don't see any guards around here." His head revolved in a half arc, then he went on: "I got half a mind to charge you with interfering in an investigation."

"What investigation? You told me the case was closed."

The jaw was working again, lips moving in and out like those of a fish after bait. "Maybe, maybe not." He blew out a puff of air. "We found some tire tracks in the brush a good four miles on the other side of the valley from Bear Lake. We're trying to get an explanation for vehicles being in the area."

In his mind, Father John could still see the flash of movement across the valley. He said, "Grover might have seen something he shouldn't have."

"You have a way of jumping to conclusions."

"But it's reasonable."

"Reasonable?" The detective gave a bark of laughter. "Sure it's reasonable. It's valuable land. Petroglyphs all over the place. Some of them on boulders anybody could haul away." He slapped the newspaper against one thigh. "This is our business, Father. I'm ordering you to stay out of it."

The agent whirled his massive frame about and cut across the field at a surprising clip to the white 4X4 in Circle Drive.

Father John retraced his steps along the third-base line. The detective could be onto something. Grover could have seen someone removing a petroglyph, and someone climbed to the ledge and hurled him off to keep him from reporting the theft. Maybe Eddie had nothing to do with it.

"Hey, Father, you see that hit?" A kid's voice broke into his thoughts.

He glanced over in time to see the hitter slide into second base. "Safe," Eldon called, moving his hands back and forth. The next kid was up.

Okay. If Eddie had nothing to do with Grover's death—his mind still searching for the logic—then why had Eddie come here? Why was he still hanging around? Why was Ali Burris deathly afraid of him?

There was the whack, followed by the sounds of a ball whistling overhead. He stood motionless, watching the outfielders running back. What had he been thinking? Trying to draw a killer to the mission—with the kids here? Slinger was right. Where were his guards?

He checked his Timex. Practice wouldn't end for another twenty minutes, but he had to get the kids out of here now. The rides would start arriving soon. A couple of pickups were already parked in front of the administration building.

"That's all for today," he called, clapping his hands to get everybody's attention. "Good practice, boys."

It took ten minutes to load the bats and balls and gloves into the canvas bags, another five minutes for him and Eldon to usher the kids—shouting, darting about—to Circle Drive. Three boys took off, struggling with the bulky equipment bags. Two other pickups had turned into the mission.

He managed to get the kids into a tight circle. "Listen up," he said. "No more practices for a couple days."

"How come, Father?" A chorus of disappointment. He caught Eldon's eye. The man knew. He'd read the *Gazette,* he'd seen the detective.

"We'll start again in a few days," he said. He hoped that was true. "Stay right here until your folks show up. Got it?"

They blinked up at him, surprise and worry mingling in the dark faces.

"See that they stay together," he said to Eldon, then he hurried across Circle Drive and down the alley next to the administration building after the boys hauling the equipment bags.

He found them in front of the storage shed behind Eagle Hall, one boy jiggling the padlock. The door swung open, and he helped them load the bags inside. He told them they were going to have to cancel practice for a while.

"Aw, Father," they said in unison.

Just for a while, he explained. They'd be back in a day

or two. Everything was fine. He didn't want them to worry. They were looking good this season.

They had already started down the alley, sneakers scratching the gravel, disappointment outlined in the slopes of their shoulders, when he turned back and snapped the padlock. It was then he saw the glint of a bumper nudged into the small space between the administration building and Eagle Hall. He moved around the shed to get a better view of the brown pickup almost completely invisible in the brush. Eddie was here.

The blood pounded in his ears as he ran back down the alley to Circle Drive. Three kids left: Josh and Enos Russet and Eldon's son, swinging on the metal handrail on the church steps, Eldon standing guard a foot away, arms folded over his chest.

"Where's your ride?" he said to the brothers.

"Dad's comin' after work." They stopped swinging and looked at him, as if to ask permission. Cowls of black hair stood up on their heads like feathered headdresses.

"Come on, boys," Eldon said. "Joseph and I are taking you home." He started toward the truck on the other side of Circle Drive, then glanced back. "You gonna be okay, Father?"

"Just get the kids out of here," he said.

"I mean, anything comes up, you call me. I can get a bunch of warriors over here real fast."

He thanked the Indian and waited until the truck had lurched through a U-turn and headed onto the straightaway out to Seventeen Mile Road, three dark heads bobbing in the rear window. Then he started toward the administration building. Eddie would be there—the most logical place.

The corridor was quiet, a mosaic of shadows and light. There was no one around.

He walked into his office on the right and hit the wall switch. Light burst over the small space. Everything the same, just as he'd lcft it two hours ago: the desk stacked high with papers and messages, the outlines of his own body pressed into the surface of the old leather chair, the two visitor chairs sitting at right angles to the desk.

He turned back to the corridor. "Come out," he called. "I know you're here."

# ‹ 23 ›

Father John could hear the sound of his own breathing over the *drip-drip* of a leaky faucet in the bathroom down the hall that bisected the corridor. He stood motionless, watching the shadows that clung to the walls. Finally: the almost imperceptible creak of a floorboard and a slight figure stepping out of a doorway. Shuffling down the corridor, hugging the shadows.

"I know who you are, Eddie," Father John said.

The man stopped. He was only a few feet away, and Father John could see him clearly—dark, flat face and broad nostrils of a Pueblo Indian; black hair slicked back behind ears that stood away from his head; pinched, worried expression. He was about five-feet-eight with narrow shoulders and thin arms that dangled at his side. The collar of his jeans jacket stood out from his scrawny neck.

"I gotta talk to you, Father." His voice was high-pitched, strained and unfamiliar. Not the voice in the confessional.

Father John motioned the Indian into his office. He moved slowly through the door, lifting and placing each foot as if he were testing the solidity of the floor beneath him. Then he stopped, looking around at the desk and chairs, the crowded bookshelves. His black ponytail hung down the back of his jeans jacket like a lone feather in a headpiece.

"Have a seat, Eddie," Father John said, knowing that the Indian would not sit down until he'd been invited.

"How d'ya know my name?" The Indian sank onto one of the chairs, a kind of gratitude in the droop of his narrow shoulders.

Father John walked over and sat down at the desk. "I heard about the fight at the Denver Indian Center."

"Them sources of yours." For the first time the mask on the brown face seemed to slip, giving way to a look of terror.

"What's your last name?"

"Ortiz."

"You're from a Pueblo?"

"Yeah. Born in Santa Clara longer ago than I can remember."

Sad, Father John thought, if it was true, and it was probably true. The man hadn't seen forty yet.

"They're gonna kill me, Father." The Indian shifted forward, fingers wrapping around the armrests. "I gotta get back to Santa Clara."

"Hold on." Father John held up one hand. "Who's going to kill you?"

"Same whites that killed Duncan. Buck Wentworth and Jimmie Delaney. They come up here looking to get a piece of Duncan and me 'cause we ripped off some tools." Eddie spoke so quietly Father John had to lean forward to catch the words.

"Let me get this straight," he said. "You and Grover both came to the res to hide out?"

"No, that ain't it, Father." The Indian was shaking his head. "Grover come first. We had a deal, me and him. I was the one took the risk getting the tools off the construction site. Wasn't easy, let me tell you. There was Wentworth—he's the meanest sonovabitch I ever seen—always watching. Wears those fancy sport coats. Always got on sunglasses. Then there was Delaney, taking orders, doing whatever the boss says. Crazy, both of 'em. And the big boss in Denver that's giving them orders, he's craziest of all. I seen Wentworth beat up a guy at the site after word come down from the big boss. Delaney helpin' out. Beat the guy with a bat till there was blood coming out of his ears 'cause they found a diamond in his boots." The man seemed to be looking at an invisible image.

"Wait a minute," Father John said. "The construction site was a diamond mine?" This was the second time somebody had mentioned diamonds in the last twenty-four hours. Vicky, last night. Now Eddie. Before that—he couldn't remember the last time. Diamonds belonged to a world he no longer inhabited, a world as alien and irrelevant as the possible life-forms in outer space.

An exasperated look came into the Indian's face. "We was dismantling a couple buildings at the mine." He glanced away. "We weren't fool enough to try making off with diamonds. Just tools laying around. Grover knew how to sell 'em for some beautiful cash. Trouble was . . ." He stopped and cleared his throat. There was the ragged sound of phlegm being rearranged.

"The bastard never give me my share."

"That's what the fight was about at the Indian Center?"

The Indian nodded. "I tell him, where's my money, man? He was drunk, and he got wild when he was drunk. Tore into me. Some guys had to pull him off, but I says, this ain't over, Grover, you can bet your sorry ass on it."

Father John was quiet a moment. "So you called the police?"

A look of astonishment flashed in the Indian's face. "I

ain't having nothing to do with the police. Just an anonymous phone call to Wentworth. I figured him and Delaney was gonna hurt Grover a lot more than me. I never figured Wentworth was good for callin' in the police."

He gave a little shrug of resignation—you could never figure everything—and went on. "Grover takes off with what he owes me. But I knew his girlfriend moved up to the res, so I figured I'd find him here. Seen her first at the convenience store. Then Grover showed up. Before I could settle with him, he disappears again. Then I seen the newspaper about him killing himself." He shook his head and glanced about the office. "What a load of shit!"

"You don't believe it?" Father John said after a moment.

"Wentworth and Delaney got him, Father." The voice was low again, almost confessional. "Threw him off the cliff."

"What makes you so sure?"

The Indian's eyes widened in astonishment. " 'Cause I seen Wentworth's white SUV in Lander last week. I was comin' out of the motel when it went by. Man, I ducked back inside fast and waited. I figured they paid Grover back for taking the equipment, now they was hanging around lookin' for me. They're still here, Father. I seen 'em yesterday." He shot a furtive glance toward the corridor, as if the spirits of the two men might be hovering there.

"Look, Eddie." Father John leaned over the desk. "You have to tell Detective Slinger." Father John knew what the man would say even before he said it. No way. He wasn't going to the police. He'd heard it a hundred times in counseling sessions, in the confessional.

The Indian was shaking his head. "That detective'll find out about the fight down in Denver and think I'm the one that went up to Bear Lake and pushed Grover off the cliff. Then he's gonna check around and find out I got a couple warrants out in Colorado, and some judge's gonna put me in jail and lose the key."

A new earnestness furrowed the man's wide forehead. "Soon's I seen the article this morning, I says to myself, the priest knows what happened to Grover. Wasn't no suicide. It was murder. You tell the detective what I said, Father. He's gonna believe you."

"You have two choices, Eddie," Father John said after a moment. "You can go with me to see Slinger, or you can keep running from Wentworth and Delaney."

The Indian regarded him. "I got another choice. You loan me some gas money, and I'm outta here. Soon's I get back to Santa Clara, I'm gonna be just fine. I'll pay you back," he hurried on. "I ain't like Grover, keeping what don't belong to me."

"You said you took the tools."

"Yeah, but . . ." He bit his lower lip. "Who cares? They got lots of money. They run a diamond company."

Father John got slowly to his feet, his gaze locked on the Indian. Vicky had said that the man killed in Denver had worked for a diamond mining company. The name? What was the name? *Baider Industries.*

"What about it, Father?" The Indian's voice cut through his thoughts.

"What's the name of the mining company?" he said.

The Indian shrugged. "Kimberly Mining. Can you let me have a couple hundred bucks?"

"Who owns it?"

"How do I know?"

"Where is it, Eddie?" Father John pushed on.

"What difference does it make?" There was a barely controlled exasperation in the man's voice. "On the Colorado–Wyoming border. Real big operation until last month when it played out and closed down." He shrugged. "That's why we was dismantling the buildings."

"Tell me something, Eddie. Is there any chance Wentworth and Delaney came here to look for a diamond deposit?"

The Indian jumped to his feet. "You don't get it, Father. They was out for revenge, 'cause we made 'em look real stupid, lifting the tools out from under their long white noses. They killed Grover, now I'm numero uno on the murder list. You gotta help me get outta here, Father."

"Here's the deal." Father John walked around and faced the man. "You go with me to see Detective Slinger, and I'll give you the gas money." He had a twenty-dollar bill and a couple of coins in his pocket. He had no idea where he'd get the rest of it.

The Indian didn't blink. "You're as tough as those other white guys," he said, turning toward the door.

"Wait," Father John said.

The Indian glanced around, a wary look creeping into his expression.

"Where are you staying?"

"Thunderbird," the man said finally.

Father John could picture the place—a remnant from the fifties, seedy and run down.

"Where all the rich folks stay." Eddie hunched his thin shoulders and ducked past the door. There was the sound of the front door opening. "Thanks for nothing," the high-pitched voice called before the door slammed shut.

Father John sat back down and, rustling through a pile of papers, pulled a yellow pad free. He found a pencil and wrote *Kimberly Mining Company* on one side of the page. Beneath that, a list of names: *Eddie Ortiz, Went-*

*worth, Delaney,* and *Grover.* He underlined Grover. Next to the name, he put *murdered.*

He started another column, with *Baider Industries* at the top, then: *Vince Lewis, wife.* Two more slashes and *murdered* after each name. He drew a line connecting the two lists and wrote: *diamonds.*

He stared at the scribbled words and tried to recall what Vicky had said about Vince Lewis: the man had wanted to give her some information about the reservation. A new idea began moving like a shadow at the edge of his mind. Maybe Wentworth and Delaney weren't looking for a couple of small-time thieves like Grover and Ortiz. Maybe they'd come to look for diamonds at Bear Lake, and Grover had spotted them and figured out what they were doing. Or maybe they thought Grover knew about the diamonds and had followed them intent on finding out what they were up to.

He pitched himself to his feet and went to the window. The mountains rose jagged and blue in the orange-tinged dusk. Northwest of the res, where the mountains dropped into a gully that allowed the sky to flow through, was Bear Lake. There was only one thing wrong with this new idea. Vicky said the diamonds were on the reservation. Bear Lake was a good forty miles away.

There was another problem: he had no proof that the two companies were connected. There could be a number of diamond mining companies in Denver.

He went back to the desk and started to pick up the phone, then hesitated. Last night Vicky had called him. He'd resolved not to call her. It was a resolve he wanted to keep. And yet . . . *There's gonna be more murders.* The words in the confessional hammered in his head.

He lifted the phone and dialed her number. When the answering machine came on, he left a short message.

Could she find out if there was any connection between Baider Industries and the Kimberly Mining Company and get back to him?

He stared at the phone after he'd hung up, wondering if he'd seized upon an excuse to get in touch with her, assuage his own concern—he'd been worrying about her since she'd called—then shrugged off the notion. If there was a connection between the companies, he'd have the first piece of hard evidence for Slinger, evidence that could explain the tire tracks the detective had already found at Bear Lake.

It was making sense, he thought, the pieces dropping into place, forming a clear image. Except . . . he had no evidence of any diamond deposits in this part of the state.

Tomorrow, he decided, after he was interviewed for the lawsuit, he'd stop by the Riverton Library and see what he could find on diamonds.

# ‹ 24 ›

"They're ready for you, Father O'Malley." The middle-aged secretary with the pinched, pale face and cropped blond hair hung up the phone that had rung a moment earlier. "Please come with me." She rose from behind a massive desk and walked over to the door across the reception area at Blackford and Lord.

Father John tossed aside a magazine, picked up his cowboy hat, and followed her down a wide corridor. She moved with authority, shoulders squared, as if she were leading a parade.

She stopped, rapped on a door, then pushed it open and motioned him into a rectangular room with an oak conference table running almost the full length. Three men sat at the far end. Arranged on the table were stacks of folders and yellow legal pads.

All three rose to their feet. "Nice to see you again, Father O'Malley." The man in the blue sport coat reached across the table and shook his hand. "Ian Blackford," he said. Father John had met him once or twice—he couldn't think where. The lawyer in a plaid shirt extended his hand and said he was Mike Lord.

"Meet Perry Hamilton from Chicago." He turned toward the man at the end. "We're providing support from the local angle, but Perry's calling the shots on the defense."

Hamilton had a grip like a steel vise, and Father John wondered what he'd be like in a courtroom, this lawyer the Society of Jesus had hired to represent Father Don Ryan.

He took the chair Mike Lord had indicated and laid his hat on the table. The lawyers sat down in unison, like a precision drill team.

"Well, Father O'Malley." Perry Hamilton laced his fingers together over the yellow legal pad. "Let me begin by allaying any worries you may have. You can be assured that the Society intends to mount a vigorous defense on behalf of Father Ryan."

"What about a fair settlement?" Father John said.

"Excuse me?" Hamilton's features rearranged themselves into a look of mock astonishment. "Do you have any idea, Father, how many lawsuits are filed against clergy?"

"I read the newspapers." Father John could feel the other lawyers' eyes on him. "Some suits are valid."

Perry Hamilton arched one eyebrow and shook his head. "Shall we proceed?" he said.

For the next hour—Father John checked his watch a couple of times—he fielded the lawyers' questions. What kind of priest was Don Ryan? Hardworking. That was the truth. How many times had Father John seen Mary Ann Williams at the mission? Once. To his knowledge, was there anything inappropriate in Father Ryan's relationship with Mary Ann Williams?

To his knowledge. Father John glanced away. In his mind was the image of Don Ryan in his study—the dropped head, the hands squeezed together between his knees. *I had an affair with her.*

"Ask Don Ryan," he said.

"We're asking you, Father." There was a sharp edge to Hamilton's voice.

"What I know was told to me in confidence, as a priest," he said. Then he held up his hand. "Why not settle, put this behind us?"

Hamilton pushed back against his chair. "Have you thought about the consequences to the mission? Try to picture your donors learning that their contributions aren't helping the Indians at all. They're paying off the priest's mistress."

Father John locked eyes with the man. "You just admitted she was Don's mistress."

A look that bordered on appreciation came into the man's face. "The burden of proof will be on her," he said. "We intend to ask a judge to hear the case. Judges are logical; they follow the law."

And you'll destroy her in court, Father John thought. You and the implacable logic of the law. He pushed his chair back, picked up his cowboy hat, and got to his feet. "I take it we're finished here," he said, starting for the door.

Father John drove through the wide streets of Riverton, a sense of futility pressing down on him like an invisible weight. Hamilton would probably win the case, and the mission wouldn't have to sell the land. Wasn't that what he wanted?

The realization left him feeling empty and dissatisfied, as if he'd conjured up a vision of what should be, only to find that it was incomplete, untrue. He'd have another talk with the Provincial. Ask him again to agree to a settlement.

He made a right onto Federal and turned onto the cement apron of a gas station. At the inside phone, he dialed the mission and tapped into his messages. Three from parishioners checking about upcoming meetings. None from Eddie or Vicky.

He pushed more quarters into the slot and dialed Vicky's law office. After two rings, Laola's voice: "Sorry, Father. Vicky's in Laramie. I knew she wouldn't be able to stay away from Wyoming." A laugh floated down the line, then: "We're still waiting to hear from the secretary of state's office on the mining companies. Vicky'll get back to you soon as she knows anything."

He thanked her and hung up, conscious of a vague disappointment that Vicky wasn't in. And something more: he had no part in her life now.

He slid back into the Toyota and melded into the light stream of traffic—a couple of pickups, a sedan—and headed north to the Riverton Library.

The redbrick building squatted in the middle of a park-like lawn that had turned emerald green in the rains. Inside was the familiar hush that reminded Father John of the neighborhood library in Boston when he was a kid, and all the libraries he'd ever done research in. Even the sense of anticipation was familiar: this was where the secrets would unfold.

He walked past the stacks set at various angles on the green carpet, past the reading tables where two elderly men curled over opened newspapers. Seated at an L-shaped desk was an attractive woman who might have been forty, with shoulder-length auburn hair framing a triangular face. She raised her eyebrows as he approached. "Haven't seen you for a while, Father."

"I believe I owe you a fine," he said, remembering the

*Plains Indians* on his desk. He pulled the twenty-dollar-bill out of his pocket and laid it down.

The librarian tapped at the computer keyboard, then pushed the bill toward him. "Keep your money for the Indian kids," she said, a mischievous light in her blue eyes. "Why do I get the feeling you aren't here to pay fines?"

"What do you have on diamonds in Wyoming?" he said.

"A new interest of yours, Father? Diamonds?"

"You might say so."

She tapped the keyboard again. "Somehow I expected you to request another history book or something on theology or spirituality. But diamonds?"

"Maybe they're related," he said. Bear Lake was a sacred, spiritual place.

"Diamonds and spirituality." She gave him a sideways look, still tapping. "How right you are. I never felt more spiritual than when I got this." She lifted her left hand and waved it in the air a moment, allowing the diamond ring on her third finger to catch the light.

"Ah, here we go." Leaning toward the computer screen now, where columns of black type scrolled downward. The scrolling stopped. She jotted three titles on a notepad, tore off the page, and handed it to him.

"You can find these in the natural history section"—a nod toward the bookshelves—"while I get you a monograph."

In a couple of minutes he'd found three books that looked promising and settled at one of the nearby tables. He opened the book titled *Wyoming Minerals,* written twenty years ago by a man with numerous letters after his name. He located "diamonds" in the index and turned to a page with a full-color map of Wyoming. Clusters of tiny white arrows pointed to the locations of diamond mines. None in central Wyoming.

He opened the next book and read a brief chapter on diamonds found in Wyoming. Superior crystals, including a faceted fifteen-point-six-carat gemstone cut from a twenty-nine-carat rough stone, the largest diamond mined in North America. More than one hundred and thirty thousand other diamonds produced. Deposits found in kimberlite pipes—columns of igneous rock injected into the earth's crust four hundred million years ago, bringing up diamonds from depths of one hundred and fifty to two hundred kilometers. Other minerals could also be found in the pipes—pyrope almondine garnet, olivine, sapphire, chromium diopside, picroilmenite, chromite. Hundreds of acres in Wyoming contained kimberlite pipes, most running along the southern border. Only a few pipes in the west and north. Whole mountain ranges ran between the nearest known pipes and central Wyoming.

In the last book, Father John scanned through the chapter titled "The Great Diamond Hoax." Diamonds discovered in southwestern Wyoming in 1872. Eastern financiers enticed to invest in America's largest diamond mine. Couple of prospectors salt the area with valuable gemstones—the only gemstone-quality crystals in the deposit. Financiers too embarrassed to press charges. One of the swindlers was from Kentucky where he became a folk hero for "out—Yankeeing the Yankees."

He closed the book, aware that the librarian had set a plastic-covered manuscript on the table and moved away as quietly as she'd approached. The plastic felt cool and brittle in his hands. He read the title page. *A History of Diamonds in Wyoming,* by Charles Ferguson, who had even more letters after his name. Slowly he turned the pages, scanning the sections with titles like "Mantle

Source Rocks in the Wyoming Craton" and "Ultramafic Complexes." The information was the same. No recorded diamond deposits in central Wyoming.

He set the manuscript on top of the books. It didn't make sense. Why had Wentworth and Delaney come here? For revenge on two small-time criminals? It seemed unlikely. And Vicky was certain Baider Industries had located diamonds on the reservation. Still, the experts were in agreement.

He got up and walked to the desk, where the librarian was bent over the open pages of what looked like a reference book.

"Have you lived in the area long?" he asked.

She brought her eyes to his. A mild look of surprise played at the corners of her mouth. "Born on the family ranch on Arrow Mountain fifty miles north. My grandfather homesteaded the place."

Father John hooked the top of a nearby chair and dragged it over. He straddled the seat and wrapped his arms around the back. "Ever hear of diamonds around here?"

"Diamonds," she said, holding on to the word, as if she were tasting the brilliance. "Sure would've made life easier if Dad could've raised diamonds instead of cattle."

"Does that mean the answer is no?"

She tilted her head back and stared at him. "We happen to be about two hundred miles from the nearest diamond mine."

He thanked her and was about to stand up when she said, "People do like to get their hopes up, though."

He wrapped his arms around the chair again. "What do you mean?"

"I was just thinking . . ." She paused, her gaze on some point across the library. "A ranch hand who worked for

Dad when I was a kid used to take off for days at a time to go prospecting, he said, but Dad always suspected he was on a drunk. One day he showed up and claimed he'd struck it rich. Said he'd found a diamond lying on the ground up in the Shoshone forest. We never saw the diamond, of course, but it was the last we saw of him. Took off right in the middle of calving season."

Father John didn't say anything. The Shoshone National Forest was west of Bear Lake. "When was this?"

"Thirty years ago." She shrugged and pulled her mouth into a thin line, as if she regretted having told him. "There was nothing to it. He probably found a sparkling crystal or got drunk and started seeing visions. If he'd found a real diamond, there would have been people crawling all over the forest looking for more." She leaned over the desk. "What's all this sudden interest in diamonds?"

He stood up and pushed the chair back in place. The last thing he wanted was to start a diamond rumor. "I'm thinking about doing some prospecting," he said. "The mission could use a diamond mine."

He thumped a knuckle on the edge of the desk, winked at her, and started for the door, almost regretting the remark. Now, instead of a diamond rumor, there'd probably be a rumor that the pastor at St. Francis had a wild imagination, maybe he'd even started drinking again.

He drove back through town, past the bungalows and ranch houses with trees budding in the yards, past the strip malls and corner gas stations, and out onto the highway, moisture flecking the windshield like tiny diamonds. The librarian's story contradicted the experts. A ranch hand had found a diamond.

A ranch hand who was a drunk. That was a problem. Drunks could see visions. He'd seen snakes once, and flashes of light. Never diamonds. But if the ranch hand *had* found a diamond in the Shoshone forest, it was possible diamonds could be found at Bear Lake.

By the time he drove into the mission, raindrops the size of quarters were plopping on the windshield. He parked close to the administration building and ran up the steps. The minute he stepped inside, the clouds opened, and a hard rain crashed against the windows. The thunder was directly overhead, like cannons firing on the roof. He hung his jacket and cowboy hat on the coattree and checked the answering machine. No new messages.

In the directory, he found a listing for the Thunderbird Motel and dialed the number. The thunder seemed farther away, like a battalion moving out onto the plains. On the third ring, a man answered, and Father John asked to speak to Eddie Ortiz.

A buzzing noise sounded, followed by the man's voice again: "He answer?"

"No," Father John said, irritated. The man must know there was no answer.

"Guess he's out."

"Is his truck gone?"

"Jesus." It sounded like a gasp. "Hold on."

Another minute passed, then: "I see that wreck still in the parking lot. Son of a bitch is probably sleeping."

"Thanks." Father John hung up. The truck was there; Eddie could be too scared to answer the phone and possibly tip off Wentworth and Delaney that he was in the room.

He jumped up, grabbed his jacket and hat again, and headed back out into the rain.

# ‹ 25 ›

Thunderbird Motel. The red-and-blue sign, blurred in the rain, hovered over the flat roof of a strip mall. Father John drove through the parking lot to the rear, where a yellow stuccoed building with cookie-cutter-identical doors and windows stood next to the alley. A last-chance place, he thought. Whole families squeezed into tiny rooms—Indians, derelicts, drugged-out teen-agers, and people who were hiding out, like Eddie.

He parked next to the brown pickup in front of a door at the far end. Pulling down his cowboy hat, he made his way around a puddle that had replaced a slab of concrete and pounded on the door. Rain drummed around him, nearly obliterating the faint television noise coming from inside. He knocked again, then stepped to the window and peered through the slit in the curtains. Lamplight shone over the mussed bed, the dresser with food cartons scattered over the top.

He walked along the building, dodging the water that poured off the overhang and spattered the concrete, and let himself through the door marked OFFICE in smudged block letters on the glass pane. Odors of damp cigarette smoke and stale coffee rushed around him. A middle-aged man with gray bushy hair that matched his eyebrows sat behind the counter that divided the small room.

"Yeah?" The man pulled his eyes away from the television on a metal shelf in one corner.

"I'm looking for Eddie Ortiz."

"You the guy that called a while ago?"

Father John nodded.

"Last room thataway." The man gestured with his head toward the opposite end of the motel.

"He doesn't answer."

"Must've gone out for a beer."

"His pickup's still in front."

The man gave a noncommittal shrug.

"Let's check the room," Father John said. "I want to make sure he's okay."

The man eyed him a moment, making up his mind. Finally he said, "Who'd you say you are?"

Father John gave his name and said he was from the mission.

"Oh, yeah. The Indian priest." The bushy eyebrows rose in a kind of recognition.

"What about the room?"

A half second passed before the man slid off the stool, almost disappearing behind the high counter. There were sounds of a drawer opening and shutting, keys rattling. He walked around the counter. A short, stocky man in a white T-shirt with wide suspenders that rode over his protruding belly and hooked into the belt of dark, rumpled pants. Without saying a word—metal key ring jangling— he opened the door and went outside.

Father John caught up and led the way. The man's sneakers made a squishy sound on the wet pavement behind him. At the door in front of the brown pickup, Father John waited while the man jammed a key into the lock and nudged the door open with one foot.

Father John moved past and went inside. The room was empty. The bed looked as if Eddie had just crawled out of it, leaving behind piles of sheets and blankets. A soap opera flickered on the television set in one corner.

He checked the bathroom: a towel wadded on the vinyl floor that was peeling back from the base of the tub, a shaving kit on the back of the toilet.

Next he flung open the closet door, every muscle in his body tense with the expectation of finding Eddie Ortiz crumpled on the floor like the towel. Except for a shirt and jacket that dangled from wire hangers, the closet was empty.

"Like I said, he went out." The manager was planted in the doorway, jiggling the keys, bored and impatient.

"Has anybody else been looking for him? Did you see anyone?"

"Hey." The man rolled his shoulders. "I just take the money at the zoo. I don't tend the animals."

Father John walked over. "Listen, you . . ." He had to stop himself from saying "moron." "When Ortiz comes back, you tell him to call me. Father O'Malley at St. Francis. It's important. You got that?"

The man blinked up at him, then stepped backward, across the walkway and into the rain that poured off the overhang and turned the white T-shirt gray against his shoulders. He jerked forward, one hand brushing at the wet shirt, and took off in the direction of the office, moving fast, sneakers slapping on the concrete.

Father John got into the Toyota and negotiated his way back through the parking lot and out onto the street, where he jammed down the accelerator, willing the old pickup to go faster. He drove north through Lander, staring past the wipers moving back and forth, back and forth, taking the intersections as the lights turned red, the voice in the confessional loud in his head: *There's gonna be more murders.*

He made a left into the parking lot that wrapped around the convenience store where he'd met Ali a couple days ago. The Toyota's tires squealed to a stop near the entrance. He jumped out and pushed through the double-glass doors, taking in the whole store at a glance: the young woman herding two kids past the candy racks, the red-faced, bald-headed man at the counter where the girl had been.

"I'm looking for Ali Burris." He walked over to the counter.

"Well, now . . ." The man's thick fingers drummed on the glass countertop. "Better get in line. Lots of people wanna find that little Indian gal."

"When do you expect her?"

"Who can say?" He shrugged. The tapping harder now. "Supposed to be here twenty minutes ago. You see her anywhere?" He gave a mock look around the store.

"I'm Father O'Malley from the reservation," Father John said. "Ali could be in trouble. Have you tried calling her?"

"Now, if I had a number, I'd be on the goddamned phone, wouldn't I? Telling her to get her ass over here. Got me a meeting I'm supposed to be at. It don't make me happy to hang around waiting for her to come dragging in here whenever she gets good and ready. Time don't mean nothing to them Indians."

Father John struggled to ignore the remark. "Tell Ali to call me at St. Francis when she comes in," he said.

"Oh, I'm gonna have a lot of things to tell that bit—" The man bit his lower lip over the word. The red in his cheeks deepened. "I ever see her again, that is."

Father John started for the door, then turned back. "What do you mean, I should get in line? Who else is looking for Ali?"

The man shook his head, as if the answer was obvious. "Couple boyfriends come around. White guys she picked up in Denver, my guess. One of 'em comes in here twirling his sunglasses, even though it's raining cats and dogs outside, like he was a hotshot movie producer. Wanted to know where Ali was."

Father John stepped back to the counter, conscious of the tension gathering inside him. "When?"

"Maybe thirty minutes ago. Just before she was supposed to come in. I told him to hang around, she'd be showing up. Sure got that wrong." He shrugged again.

"What did the guy look like?" Father John heard the tightness in his voice.

"Like anybody." He rolled his eyes to the ceiling. "Some guy, that's all. Couple inches taller than me— about six feet, dark hair, blue sport coat, fancy loafers. Twirling those sunglasses."

Father John drew in a long breath. The tension was like a pit in his throat that he couldn't swallow. The description matched Eddie's description of Buck Wentworth.

"What about the other guy? You said there were two."

"Stayed outside." The man nodded toward the window and the parking lot beyond. "I seen him out there. Had on a red baseball jacket, that's all I know."

That would be Delaney. The pieces were falling into place now.

"What were they driving?"

"What's this all about?"

"Just tell me."

The man rolled his eyes again and shrugged. "One

sweet SUV, white, riding high." He leaned over the counter and shot a glance toward the woman and kids still hovering around the candy section. "You wanna know what got me?"

He paused, then said something about not being able to figure out what a couple of white guys in an expensive rig like the SUV seen in that little Indian gal.

Father John heard only part of it, a buzz of background noise to his own thoughts. Wentworth and Delaney had shown up just as Ali was due to come in. They were waiting for her in the parking lot. She never reached the store.

Okay, he told himself. You don't know that for a fact. Think rationally, logically. Eddie and the girl aren't stupid. They could have spotted the white SUV earlier and gone to the res together to hide out a while. They could both be safe.

"What else did he say?" Father John kept his voice low, controlled.

"Funny thing." The man had begun tapping the counter again. "Just asked when she was supposed to be here, then went on outside. Didn't leave no messages, if that's what you mean. Like he was gonna see her before I did."

Father John spun around and pushed through the door. Wentworth and Delaney were mopping up, just as Delaney had said in the confessional. Mopping up the last two people who might alert the sheriff and the tribes about a secret diamond deposit at Bear Lake.

He found a quarter in his jeans pocket and pushed it into the slot in the phone on the brick wall outside. Huddling out of the rain, he dialed the sheriff's office and asked for Matt Slinger.

"Sorry. Detective Slinger's not in."

"Then put another detective on," Father John said. He

gave his name and told the operator it was an emergency.

The line went quiet. Behind him, the rain beat on the parking lot, and passing cars splashed through the puddles in the street. Finally a man's voice: "Detective Kowalski. What can I do for you, Father O'Malley?"

He leaned closer to the phone and told the detective about Eddie Ortiz and Ali Burris, taken captive about thirty minutes ago by two men from Denver—Buck Wentworth and Jimmie Delaney. They were driving a white SUV.

"Hold on. I'm writing as fast as I can." A hollow sound filled the line. Finally the detective said, "You say the two Denver guys took the man and woman by force?"

"That's exactly what I'm saying. They were both afraid of them." Father John drew in a long breath. There wasn't time to explain. "Look," he said, trying to separate what he'd heard in the confessional from everything else he knew. "Eddie told me that Wentworth and Delaney followed him and Duncan Grover from Denver." *Careful.* "Eddie believes the Denver guys killed Grover."

"We talkin' about the Indian that committed suicide?"

"It wasn't a suicide," Father John said. He heard the exasperation in his tone. "Slinger's been reinvestigating Grover's death. He thinks Grover may have stumbled onto something at Bear Lake."

"Somebody helping themselves to the petroglyphs."

"The point is . . ." Dear God, there wasn't enough time to get into the possibility of a diamond deposit. "Eddie says that the two men came up here planning to kill all of them, the girl, too. They've already killed Grover. You've got to stop them before they kill the others. Shouldn't be too hard to spot a white SUV with green plates around here."

"You know how many square miles we cover here, Father? More than nine thousand. That SUV's had a half-hour start. They could be thirty miles in any direction. You got any idea where they might be heading?"

He knew. Suddenly he knew. It was logical. Logic was about patterns, and Delaney understood patterns. He'd gotten involved in murder, then come back to the sacrament that had been healing and comforting when he was younger. The priest would protect him, he knew, but the priest would also do whatever he could to prevent other murders. Delaney would send a message, like a neon sign flashing in the rain. *Look at the pattern, Father O'Malley, and stop the murders.*

Grover's death looked like a suicide; Eddie and Ali would look like suicides, too. Grover had died at Bear Lake. The others would die there. Two more Indians imitating Grover, choosing to die in a sacred place. It would even seem logical to the outside world.

"They're on their way to Bear Lake," he said. "Wentworth and Delaney intend to throw Eddie and the girl off the cliffs, just as they did Grover."

"How d'ya know all this?"

"Listen to me, Detective!" He was shouting now. "You've got to get some officers out there right away!" He slammed the phone down and made a dash through the rain to the Toyota. Thunder cracked in the distance, and lightning lit up the ridges of the mountains. The storm was centered to the north, over Bear Lake, he realized. The spirits were angry.

The engine burst into life, and he pressed down the accelerator and pulled out into the street. He glanced at his watch. Almost five-thirty. It would be dark soon. Within moments he was speeding north on Highway 287 toward Bear Lake.

# ‹ 26 ›

Vicky watched the black sedan in the rearview mirror. It had been there on I-25, on the exit ramp to I-80. She had first noticed it about ten miles north of Denver. Always the same distance behind. Other vehicles moved in between, but when they pulled away, the sedan was still there.

She was getting paranoid, she told herself, imagining the sedan was following her. First Vince Lewis murdered, then Jana Lewis. She was nervous. A black sedan had killed Lewis.

Vicky pressed hard on the gas pedal, picking up speed—the needle hovering at eighty, the gray asphalt rolling toward her. She glanced into the rearview mirror. The sedan had dropped back until it was nothing more than a dark smudge on the horizon.

She took a deep breath and relaxed her grip on the steering wheel. Traffic was light. A few cars and trucks and semis in the oncoming lane. A line of semis ahead. On either side of the highway, the vast, limitless plains spread as far as she could see, merging into the sky. She could make out the dips of the arroyos, the gentle rise of the plateaus, covered with wild grasses raked by the wind. The land was part of her, in her blood—a blood memory passed down from the ancestors. No matter where she went, she could never leave the plains behind.

She'd filed the brief with the appellate court this morning, then arranged to take the rest of the day off to drive to Laramie, wondering now if the appointment with Charles Ferguson was an excuse to escape onto the plains. The meeting would probably be a waste of time. The Wyoming Department of Environmental Quality had confirmed that no letters of authorization had been issued to take samples of soil on state land in central Wyoming. Nor had any licenses to explore been issued. She'd also contacted the state land office. No mineral leases had been granted to explore for diamonds in central Wyoming, and no permits issued to mine diamonds there.

Vicky gripped the wheel against the force of air from a passing semi. Tiny specks of dirt and rock pinged on the windshield. Nathan Baider's men could have found a deposit and could be working it without the necessary legal steps. The penalty was high—ten thousand dollars a day—but Wyoming was a big state. She doubted the state had enough mining inspectors to cover the vast expanse of undeveloped areas in central Wyoming alone. Lewis had died trying to tell her something. She owed it to the man to find out what it was. She owed it to her people.

The Laramie roofs shimmered on the plains ahead, and Vicky let up on the accelerator and again glanced in the rearview mirror. The black sedan was there. She felt her heart take a little jump.

Still there as she took the exit onto the flat wide pavement leading into town and drove past the car dealerships and motels and box stores that bunched closer and closer together as she neared the center.

"You're not the only one going to Laramie," she said

out loud, startled at the fear in her voice. She shot through a yellow light and passed a pickup, pulling away from the sedan. Another glance in the mirror. The sedan had disappeared.

The campus came into view on the right, two- and three-story redbrick buildings surrounded by lawns and concrete walkways and cottonwoods that had probably been there in the Old Time. Through the trees, she could see the yellow-brick geology building.

"Can't miss us," Ferguson had said on the phone. "We're the only yellow building around here."

She found a vacant parking place on a residential block and walked back to campus. There was an instant when she thought she saw the black sedan in the next block, but then it was gone.

Inside the building, she studied the directory a moment before making her way down a narrow corridor to a door with CHARLES FERGUSON printed in black letters below the glass pane. She knocked.

"Come on in." The friendly voice on the phone yesterday, as open as the Wyoming plains, gave her a sense of normality and security.

She stepped inside and stopped. The room looked like a storeroom, with cartons, books, and papers crammed onto shelves against the walls and various-sized glass containers filled with specimens of rock and soil stacked on the metal cases that jutted into the room.

A slim, fit-looking man rose from the desk wedged beneath the window. Outside was the redbricked view of another building. "Professor Ferguson?" she said.

"Most folks call me Charlie," he said, motioning her forward. He looked about thirty-five, with short-trimmed brown hair and the ruddy complexion of a cowboy who spent his days herding cattle. He wore blue jeans and a plaid shirt, the sleeves rolled up around muscular fore-arms. Instead of cowboy boots, he had on brown, lace-up hiking boots.

"I'm Vicky Holden." She picked a path around the metal cases and held out her hand.

"Pleased to meet you." He gave her a wide friendly smile that accentuated the tiny squint lines at the corners of his light eyes. When he shook her hand, she could feel the strength in his grip.

He nodded toward the chair next to the desk and told her to have a seat. On the wall above was a map of Wyoming similar to the map in Nathan Baider's office. Pins with various-colored heads—red, blue, yellow—dotted the periphery. There were no pins in the center.

"I appreciate your taking the time to see me," she said, settling on the hardwood chair.

The professor sat down in an oak swivel chair and regarded her a moment. "You're not the first woman I've met who's interested in diamonds."

"I'm only interested in the prospecting part," she said.

"Well, now . . ." He smiled. "That could be a first. How can I help you?"

Vicky took in a deep breath. It still took her by surprise the way white people got right down to business. She said, "Do you know of any diamond deposits in central Wyoming? Any reason for prospectors to look for deposits on the reservation?"

"The reservation?" Ferguson's eyebrows shot up, and she braced herself for a firm "no." Hoped for the answer, she realized. She could stop wasting her time and start believing that Lewis's death had nothing to do with her people.

Ferguson cleared his throat, a professor about to deliver a lecture. "Mining companies," he began, "usually deploy prospecting resources in areas with the best chance of success, which would be near known diamond deposits. As you can see"—he waved toward the map—"most deposits are on the southern border. Several companies operate mines there. The biggest is Baider Industries, which owns three mines. Although . . ." He paused, as if he'd just remembered something. "The Kimberly closed down its operations last month. Mine played out."

"The Kimberly!" Vicky stood up and peered at the map a moment. She'd seen the Kimberly Mine on another map—in Nathan Baider's office. And yesterday John O'Malley had left a message, wanting to know about the Kimberly Mining Company. She'd asked Laola to run a check on the company with the secretary of state's office. She wouldn't have to wait for the report. The company was a subsidiary of Baider Industries.

"Is it important?" Ferguson was staring at her.

"I don't know," she said after a moment. She was thinking that if the Kimberly Mine had played out, Nathan Baider could be desperate to find another deposit. He was anxious to produce more diamonds that could be certified on the world market. Maybe he got reckless and sent a crew to the reservation without taking the time to work through the tribal bureaucracy and secure the legal permits. Maybe . . .

Except there were no pins with rounded, colored heads in the center of the map.

She turned to the professor who was watching her, questions mingling with the concern in his face. "Are you telling me there aren't any diamond deposits on the reservation?"

"We don't know that," he said.

Vicky sat back down. "What do you mean?"

Ferguson rearranged his angular frame in the chair and

drew in a long breath. "It has to do with the peculiar geographical formation underlying Wyoming," he began. "The entire state happens to be underlaid by a craton that is intruded by the largest field of kimberlite pipes in the United States. The pipes erupted like volcanoes about four hundred million years ago from ninety to one hundred and twenty miles below the earth's surface, bringing up diamonds and other minerals. So far we've recorded forty diatremes, the upper portion of the volcanic structures, in Wyoming. Hold on." He jumped up and disappeared in the maze of metal cases. In a moment he was back. "Kimberlite rock," he said, handing her a chunk of dark gray rock that resembled solidified lava. It was lightweight and dense.

"Hard to believe diamonds come from such ugly ducklings," he said, dropping back in the swivel chair, a fond gaze on the rock in her hand. "Some geologists believe Wyoming will someday be one of the world's richest diamond producers, right up there with Africa."

Vicky glanced up at the map of Wyoming, a vast, empty space of mountain ranges and plains. "Why the reservation?" she asked, locking eyes with him again. "If diamonds can be found anywhere, why would a mining company decide to look on the res?"

Ferguson shrugged. "There's always the possibility that someone stumbled on a pipe. Sometimes prospectors find other minerals that come from the pipes—pyrope almondine garnets, sapphires, and chromium diopside, which is the color of emeralds. They wash them out of a creekbed, then trace them upstream until they locate the kimberlite pipe they washed from. They start digging. Take test samples of earth, looking for diamonds."

Vicky was acutely aware of the maze of metal shelves around the room, the glass containers of rocks and minerals and residue—the earth reduced to small physical parts. So different from the way she always thought of the earth: a whole being with its own spirit. And yet, for this scientist—the light eyes seldom leaving the kimberlite rock in her hand—the earth's spirit was in each small part: diamonds, trace minerals, ugly-duckling rocks.

"What about trace minerals?" she said. "Have they been found on the reservation?"

Ferguson didn't say anything. He reached past her, retrieved a small vial the size of a prescription bottle, and handed it to her. "Garnets and sapphires," he said. "I washed them out of the creekbed there." He pointed to a spot on the map that Vicky guessed was about fifty miles north of the reservation.

She held the bottle up to the window, turning it slowly in her hand. A layer of red and blue grains sparkled in the light. Then she stood up and studied the area he had pointed to. Dubois to the north, Table Mountain and Indian Meadows farther south, creeks crisscrossing the area. To the west, the direction from which the creeks flowed out of the mountains, was the Shoshone forest and, over a ridge, Bear Lake, a place of spirits, important to her people.

She sank onto her chair and closed her eyes. The pieces of the puzzle were beginning to form a clear image. She'd assumed that Vince Lewis had wanted to tell her something about the reservation. She was wrong. Nathan Baider had found diamonds at Bear Lake. A diamond mine would drive the spirits away. The Arapahos and Shoshones would lodge complaints with the state, file lawsuits, do everything possible to protect the area, which explained why Baider had to work in secret. Vince Lewis had died trying to warn her so that she could warn the tribes, and his wife must have known what was going on.

She must have confronted Nathan Baider. If Duncan Grover had come upon the secret, it would explain why he had been killed.

"Are you all right?"

Vicky's eyes snapped open. Charlie Ferguson was bending over her, as if he might take her pulse, his own eyes narrowed with worry.

"I'm okay," she managed. She made herself take a long breath. "Suppose Baider Industries located a diamond deposit at Bear Lake. What would be the next step?"

Charlie Ferguson looked startled. "Bear Lake Valley? That would be highly controversial. They might want to keep it secret. Wouldn't want tourists and rock hounds trampling the area. They should get a mineral lease and authorization, but they might not. They might want to see what they'd found first. Dig a prospect pit about twelve hundred feet deep and take out a few thousand pounds of rock. The average diamond yield is point-zero-five carats to seven carats per ton of rock. If the sample rocks showed gemstone-quality stones, they'd want to make a bulk commercial test with about ten thousand tons of rock. At some point they'd probably file for a mining permit."

"How much time are we talking about?"

"An established mining company that knows the ropes—"

"Like Baider Industries," Vicky cut in.

The man shrugged. "Let's just say the process would be smooth."

"A mine could be operating before anyone realized what was going on?"

"Possibly."

Unless someone like Vince Lewis decided to blow the whistle, Vicky was thinking. She turned back to the map: a blue-and-green blur with red, yellow, and white pins jumping out at her. After a moment she realized the professor had sat down, and she took her own chair.

"How large is a diatreme?"

"Anywhere from a few acres of surface area to a mile in diameter."

"How can I find the kimberlite pipe in Bear Lake Valley?" she said.

Ferguson exhaled a long stream of air. "You could try panning for trace minerals downstream from the valley . . ." He hesitated. "You could hire a plane to fly over the valley and do photo imaging, the way DeBeers locates new deposits in the interior of Australia. A very expensive process, I might add."

Vicky shifted forward, a sense of excitement gathering inside her. "What about satellite imaging? Could satellite sensors detect a kimberlite pipe?"

The professor shrugged. "Sensors can detect the color of your hair," he said. "Problem lies in interpreting the data. It takes highly trained geologists. Some work in government labs. Others are at commercial satellite companies that sell the imaging data."

Vicky stood up and swung her bag over one shoulder. "You've been very helpful," she said.

"I'm afraid you're on the wrong track." Charlie Ferguson was on his feet next to her. "I've known Nathan Baider for years. If he found a new deposit in central Wyoming, he'd notify our office."

"You said a mining company would want to keep a new deposit secret." Vicky kept her eyes on his.

"From the public and other mining outfits," the man said, "not from our office. It would be a significant find, the first pipe identified in the area. I can't believe Nathan wouldn't have let us know."

Vicky drew in a deep breath. "The pipe's there," she said after a moment. "I intend to prove it."

"How do you propose to do that?"

"The same way an oil and gas company proved methane gas on the Navajo reservation." She shook the man's hand and thanked him again, ignoring the puzzled look that had come into his eyes.

Vicky walked back across the campus, pulling her cell phone from her bag as she went and punching in the number for Jacob Hazen's office. There was a roll of thunder in the distance, a speckle of rain. After she'd talked her way past the secretary—"Don't-tell-me-Mr.-Hazen's-in-a-meeting this is an emergency"—the voice of the Navajo lawyer burst through the line, as loud and clear as if he were in one of the buildings she was walking by.

"Tell me, Jacob," she said, launching into the reason for the call, marveling at the white habits she'd picked up, "who interpreted the satellite data on the new methane gas field?"

There was a pause on the other end. "This have to do with the brief?"

"The brief is at the appellate court," she said, letting herself into the Bronco. Rain pecked at the windshield.

The man's sigh sounded like a gust of wind through a tunnel. "Geophysicist at Global Visions, the satellite company we bought the data from. Name is Dave Hendricks."

Vicky extracted a notepad and pen from her bag. Thunder came again, causing static on the line. She scribbled down the name of the company. Probably in New Mexico or Arizona, close to Navajo land.

"They're here in Denver," the lawyer said, as if he'd tuned in to her thoughts. "Out at the tech center."

Denver. She glanced past the windshield at the black clouds in the north, over the reservation, and breathed a silent prayer of thanksgiving to the spirits that guarded the world. "Can you get me an appointment this afternoon?"

"This afternoon?"

"I can be there at four," she said, checking the dashboard clock. It was a little after twelve.

"What's this about?"

"About a mining company that's going to destroy a sacred place."

"I don't know, Vicky." Another sigh mingled with the static. "A sacred place, you say?"

"Bear Lake in central Wyoming."

"The place of the spirits," the lawyer said after a pause. "Okay. I'll ask Hendricks if he can help out. Don't be late."

Vicky hit the end button, then dialed her firm. After a moment Laola was on the line. "Vicky Holden's office."

"Any messages?"

"Secretary of state faxed over a report. You'll never guess who owns the Kimberly Mining Company."

"Baider Industries."

Silence. A second passed before Laola said, "Soon's the report came in, I tried to call Father John, but he was out. I left a message. Oh, one more thing. Lucas called. Wanted to make sure dinner's still on tonight."

Vicky told the secretary she'd see her tomorrow and pressed a couple of buttons. Lucas's voice mail clicked on. "I'm running late, Lucas," she said, cradling the phone into her shoulder, starting the engine and steering the Bronco into the traffic moving away from campus. She was always late with her children, she thought. Always behind someplace where she should have been.

"It'll be seven-thirty before I can get to the restaurant." She paused. "I'm looking forward to it."

As she took the on-ramp to I-80, she saw the black sedan in the side mirror. The vehicle was coming up the ramp.

She jammed down the gas pedal and passed a semi, then another, the Bronco shaking beneath her, her hands trembling on the rim of the steering wheel. Then she swung into the passing lane again. Another semi dropped behind, then a truck and sedan. The highway ran ahead. Another semi, as small as a child's toy, was framed in the gray sky.

She was flooring the gas pedal now, racing toward the semi, putting as much distance as she could between the Bronco and the black sedan behind her. She could hear the thunder in the distance.

# ‹ 27 ›

The storm had broken loose, washing great sheets of water over the pickup as Father John drove north across the reservation. Thunder crashed overhead, followed by jagged flashes of lightning that lit up the air a moment before the haze closed in again. The pavement ahead shimmered in the headlights. Occasionally other headlights rose out of the haze, and another vehicle blurred past. He could barely make out the shadows of the foothills to the west, but to the east there was nothing. He might have been driving on the edge of the earth.

Another truck passed, and the Toyota started to hydroplane, flying through the rain. He let up on the gas pedal until the tires gripped the pavement again.

He realized the turnoff to Bear Lake had flashed outside his window, but he was already past. He hit the brakes. The Toyota skidded sideways before stopping broadside across the pavement. He pulled the steering wheel left and drove back, peering past the wipers for the dirt road into the mountains.

It rose into the headlights. He slowed for the turn and started winding up a narrow, muddy path. The rear wheels spun sideways, then found a purchase that sent the Toyota plunging ahead, pine branches raking the sides. There were fresh tracks—deep impressions filled with water. Wentworth's SUV, he thought.

The road curved through a half circle and emerged into the mountain valley, with scrub brush and willows bent under the rain. The lake had to be close. He slowed down to get his bearings. After a moment he saw the gray surface of the lake rising to meet the rain.

He followed the road around the shoreline and stopped near the clump of willows where he'd parked a few days ago. There was no sign of the SUV. He hesitated. He could be wrong. Wentworth and Delaney could have taken their captives somewhere else; there were hundreds of miles of open spaces around. They could be anywhere.

He didn't think so. They were here. It was the logical place.

The moment he turned off the headlights, he was enveloped in the gray haze. He found a flashlight under the seat. Dead. He knocked it against the palm of his hand until it sprang to life and sent a thin thread of light flickering over the windshield and dashboard. Then he got out, pulled his cowboy hat forward, and started through the willows, flashing the light about, searching for the footpath to the cliffs lost in the clouds above.

The light shone over something white in the branches. He pulled them aside. Tire tracks through the sodden underbrush led to the white SUV. A few feet ahead was the opening in the brush where the path started.

Rain beat against his jacket and ran off the brim of his hat as he started up the path. The flashlight cast a thin column of light ahead. He followed the footprints in the mud—different-sized prints overlapping one another. Ahead, the smaller prints slid into a flattened area near the trees. Ali must have fallen. Fallen and been dragged back to her feet. The small prints loped from side to side, as if the girl had been stumbling.

Let me get there in time, he prayed. He was half jogging now, pounding his boots hard into the slippery mud. He would have a chance with Delaney, he tried to convince himself. The man retained a semblance of morality, a sense of right and wrong that had driven him to the confessional. He did not want to kill again. But the boss—Wentworth—was a cold-blooded killer. It was Delaney he would have to appeal to. And Delaney was logical.

The thunder sounded like tanks rumbling through the sky. Lightning turned the air white and sent a charge through the earth that he could feel reverberating inside him. He was in an opening, with the trees falling away, when the lightning flashed again. For the briefest moment he saw the petroglyph shining on the cliff above—human looking, eyes all-seeing, hands raised in benediction. He was not alone. The spirits were here, the messengers of the Creator.

He climbed faster, light from the flashlight bouncing ahead. With every flash of lightning, he searched the cliffs above for the ledge, for some movement, some sign of the two men and their captives. There was nothing, only the petroglyph urging him onward.

He started up the boulder field, the climb steeper now, hand over hand. He jammed the flashlight into his jacket pocket and grabbed blindly at the rain-slicked boulders, depending on the lightning to see. His boots slipped backward, and a large rock came loose under his hand. For a moment he thought the boulder field would start rolling downhill, carrying him along.

Suddenly he saw a light in the rain above. He kept climbing, moving slowly now, feeling the way, trying to catch his breath as he pushed on. His chest felt tight, his throat constricted. The ledge was a few feet above. He pulled himself up onto a narrow path, keeping one hand on the flat face of the cliff for balance. Below, the mountainside dropped into the darkness.

The thunder came again, like a blast of dynamite that made the cliff tremble beneath his hand. In the lightning that followed, he made out three figures on the ledge. The petroglyph above was chalk white.

Out of the corner of his eye, he saw the shadow lunging at him. Instinctively he backed into the cliff. The sharp edges of rock stabbed through his jacket and into his skin. When the blow came, it was like an explosion inside his head.

There was an instant, no more, when his whole consciousness collapsed into pain that ran like a river down his spine. He felt his legs dissolving beneath him, and he clawed at the face of the cliff to stay upright in the darkness closing around.

# ‹ 28 ›

It was quitting time at the Denver Tech Center. Techies in jeans and khakis, a few managers in shirts and ties, poured from the glass-and-concrete buildings, down the walkways that curved through manicured lawns. Vicky spotted the sign for Global Vision and parked in the lot.

She rode the glass-enclosed elevator to the tenth floor and stepped out into a carpeted reception area with windows that curved around the periphery like the cockpit of a spaceship. Beyond the windows, the clouds seemed close enough to touch.

"May I help you?" A young woman with long, dark hair that hung down the front of her white blouse looked up from a computer screen.

"I have an appointment with Dr. Hendricks." Vicky handed her business card across the desk.

"He's expecting you." The woman gave her a welcoming smile and lifted the phone. "Ms. Holden to see you," she said into the receiver. Another smile as she set the phone into place.

"Ms. Holden?"

Vicky swung around. A slim man in his mid-thirties, about six feet tall, dressed in khakis and a yellow polo shirt, came toward her, hand extended. His palm was rough against hers, like the palms of men who spent time outdoors.

"Come on back." He waved her through a doorway and into a large room filled with cubicles. "Here we are." A hand shot out at her side and ushered her into a cubicle on the right.

It was small: a couple of chairs, bookcases crammed with books and cartons, a desk in front of the window. An outsized computer monitor took up most of the desk's surface.

"Make yourself at home." He pulled a chair over to the edge of the desk and dropped into the other chair in front of the monitor. "Jacob tells me you're looking into the possibility of diamond deposits in the Bear Lake Valley," he said. "Wonderful place." His expression took on a far-away look. "Spent a couple weeks hiking up there two years ago, looking at the petroglyphs. You can sense something special about the place. Be a shame to see the valley ruined by a mine."

"My people won't let it happen." Vicky felt the beginning of trust for this white man.

"Arapahos."

She nodded.

He turned to the computer and began clicking the mouse. A haze of gray, blue, and green flowed onto the screen, like an impressionistic painting taking shape. "You're seeing a bird's-eye view of Wyoming," he said, his gaze on the colors that dissolved and re-formed. "From about four hundred miles above the earth's surface. There are the Wind River mountains below the cloud cover." He pointed to the knobs of white poking through the gray-ness. "Okay, now we're closing in on the central part of the state. I'm going to bring it up."

She was looking down on the Wind River mountains: the snow covering the high, treeless peaks, the sharp definition of cliffs, the rivers threading the area. A tiny truck was on a road. Ranch buildings, trucks, and cars scattered about a green meadow, like miniature blocks.

Slowly the image began moving eastward over the valley itself. They were skimming the tops of the junipers and piñons, swooping overhead like the eagles that guarded the area. She could see the jagged cliffs and Bear Lake nestled at the base of the slopes. "I don't see the petroglyphs," she said.

"They're here." The image stopped on the cliffs above the lake. "We're looking straight down, so we can't pick up the vertical images on the face of the cliffs."

After a moment she heard herself telling the scientist that the valley was a holy place where the spirits had chosen to live on the earth.

"I believe it," he said, moving the mouse. "Now let's go prospecting." The view was changing. The mountain slopes and pine trees gave way to meadows carpeted in grasses.

Vicky held her breath. Suppose there was no pipe. Her theory would collapse. Nothing about the deaths of Vince and Jana Lewis would make sense.

"Bingo," Hendricks said. "Here it is." He pointed to an open park. "Kimberlites are marked by vegetation anomalies. No trees in the area, and noticeably higher stands of grass, which makes the pipe susceptible to remote sensing. Also, notice the bluish earth caused by the erosion of the rocks."

There was a clicking sound, and the image was magnified. Through the brush and grass, Vicky could see the large bluish circle in the earth. The circle was enclosed by dark rocks, so different from the red-and-brown boulders in the area and the pink sandstone cliffs above.

"A kimberlite pipe," Hendricks said. "Formed from molten lava thrust up four hundred million years ago. Brought diamonds close to the surface, where human beings, real Johnny-come-latelies on the earth, found the sparkling nuggets and decided they'd look good on their bodies. Imagine. People walking around with billion-year-old rocks on their fingers." He glanced at her left hand, then looked away.

"Are there other pipes in the valley?" she said.

"We'll see." He turned back to the screen. Fifteen, twenty minutes passed. The scientist was quiet, immersed in the changing images.

"Don't find any," he said finally. "Doesn't mean they're not there. It'd take a lot of time to examine the data more closely."

The kimberlite pipe he'd found flashed back onto the screen. "Look at that." He jabbed a finger at what looked like a disturbed area in a section of the black rock. "Somebody's been working this pipe. Probably taking test samples of ore."

Vicky could feel her heart speed up. "What's the exact location?"

"Exact coordinates, here we come." Another *click-click*. Numbers appeared on the screen.

"How far is the pipe from the main road?"

Hendricks studied the numbers. "I'd say about four miles in a straight line north of the big petroglyph on the cliff. I'll print it for you." He clicked the mouse. A whirring sound started somewhere down the corridor.

"I can't tell you how much help you've been," Vicky said, rising from her chair.

The scientist was on his feet. "Hold on," he said, darting out the door. In two or three minutes he was back. He handed her a printout of the image.

"Not often I get the chance to go looking for diamonds," he said, walking her into the corridor. "I'm usually after the telltale signs of oil and coal and methane gas. Not as exciting."

She shook the man's hand and told him she could find her way out.

This is it, she thought, clutching the paper to the front of her raincoat as the elevator dropped past the other floors. She had the evidence, the motive for three murders.

She dialed Steve Clark's number as she made her way into the parking lot. It was raining lightly, the black clouds lengthening overhead. His answering machine picked up, and the familiar instruction came over the line. "Leave your name and number. I'll get back to you."

"It's Vicky." She slid inside the Bronco and turned the ignition. The engine emitted a low growl. "I have information on Vince Lewis's murder. I have to talk to you right away."

She ended the call, and at the red light on Orchard Road, she dialed St. Francis Mission. The phone started to ring as she turned onto the entrance to I-25. The green-and-white highway signs swayed overhead, and the wipers cleared twin cones on the windshield.

For the first time she noticed the black sedan in the rearview mirror. Her mouth went dry. The ringing stopped, replaced by another answering machine, another familiar voice. *Where are you, John?*

At the beep, she said, "Call me as soon as you get in. I know what's going on at Bear Lake. I know why Duncan Grover was murdered."

She clicked off, tossed the phone on the passenger seat, and swung out into the passing lane. Pressing hard on the accelerator, passing a string of cars before pulling back into the right lane. The black sedan was still there.

She turned out again, this time switching back and forth across the lanes, weaving through the traffic, the windshield wipers squealing like trapped animals.

The sedan was gone. Her hands froze to the wheel. The sedan on the highway to Laramie, and now here. How could she have been so naive? She was only gathering information, she'd told herself. There was no danger. Information was always dangerous, if someone didn't want you to have it. Vince and Jana Lewis had been killed because of information.

The black sedan was in the mirror again. Suddenly it shot past, but not before she caught a glimpse of a dark-haired, middle-aged white man at the wheel, his face averted from her. The sedan passed three or four cars ahead before disappearing into the lane she was in.

The overhead signs blurred past. Colfax. Speer Boulevard. Vicky moved into the turning lane and followed the ramp that curved over the highway before dumping her onto North Speer. She made herself take several deep breaths. The sedan was gone for good this time.

# ‹ 29 ›

Vicky spotted Lucas as she drew up in front of the corner restaurant: seated behind the plate-glass window with the words ITALIAN HOME-STYLE COOKING across the top. Alone at a table draped in a white cloth, head bent over a magazine, a mug in one hand. His dark complexion, a startling contrast to the white cloth.

How handsome he was, she thought, running across the sidewalk to the entrance. How much like Ben, even the muscular contours of his shoulders under the light blue shirt.

"Hey, Mom!" He jumped to his feet the minute she stepped inside, as if he'd felt her presence. The restaurant was warm and redolent of the odors of tomato sauce and spices. The tables were full. There was a buzz of conversation, the noise of clinking dishes.

"Sorry I'm late." She shrugged out of her raincoat.

"It's okay." He came around the table, hung her coat over the stand near the door, then pushed in her chair for her. Where had he learned such things? Sometimes in the middle of the night she lay awake, trying to remember if she'd passed on to Lucas and Susan important things that had been passed on to her: be considerate, be humble, be thoughtful in all things. She could never remember for certain, and it always left her shaken with a feeling of incompleteness, of things half-finished.

"You okay, Mom?" Lucas took his chair next to her.

She nodded and gave him her best smile.

"We've been worrying about you."

Vicky waited until the waitress had taken their orders and turned away. "You and who else?" she said, instantly regretting the question.

"Talked to Dad today," Lucas said. "He says you oughta come back to the res with your own people. He'd look out for you. Too bad—"

She held up one hand. "Don't, Lucas," she said.

Silence dropped between them while the waitress delivered plates of spaghetti and meatballs, steam curling over the top. When the waitress moved away, Vicky changed the subject: "How are the job interviews?" she said, a forced lightness in her tone. She left the house early in the mornings, came home late. They'd been passing each other on the sidewalk.

"Great," he assured her.

Twirling the spaghetti around her fork, she pressed on: a series of small questions, the pleasantries exchanged by strangers. His answers were short, perfunctory, accompanied by shrugs.

Finally Lucas said, "So what's up with Laramie?"

She took a bite of spaghetti and, after a moment, told him about Charlie Ferguson, an expert on diamond deposits.

Lucas reared back. Understanding flashed in his dark eyes. "You're still trying to find out who ran that guy down." The hard note in his voice surprised her. "You're still getting involved in dangerous stuff, just like before."

"Lucas, you don't understand."

"Oh, I get it all right." He tossed his napkin onto the

table. "It doesn't matter how much Dad and Susan and I worry about you. You don't give a flying—" He curled his lips back. "You don't care about us."

"That's not true." The alarm rose like phlegm in her throat. The rest of the restaurant grew quiet. Vicky could sense the family at the next table staring at them.

"I'm not in any danger." She kept her voice low. My God, she was lying to her own son. Information was dangerous. She started to tell him about the kimberlite pipe four miles north of Bear Lake, then stopped herself. She couldn't pass on the danger to him.

"Look, Lucas," she said. "I found the evidence that proves Vince Lewis was murdered. I've left a message with Detective Clark—"

"Listen to yourself, Mom," he cut in. "You're talking about murder! You're after a murderer! What if the murderer decides to come after you? You expect us to sit back and wait for some policeman to call and say they found your body somewhere? You've got to back off." He took her hand, squeezing it hard. "Promise me you'll back off."

She cupped her other hand over her mouth a moment; she didn't want to start crying. What a sight for the people craning their necks around. Finally she said, "I'll talk to Detective Clark tomorrow."

"Don't you ever give up?" He dropped her hand, tossed his napkin across the table, and stood up. His knuckles popped white out of the brown fists clenched at his side. He leaned over her. "You can't stop, can you? You can't stay out of things that don't concern you. What is it? The danger? Is that what you love?"

"Don't, Lucas." She reached toward him, but he stepped back.

"That's it, the danger. It's like a drug, and you're addicted. It must be a real high, outwitting killers, dodging them before they can kill you. And you left Dad because he was addicted to alcohol!" He gave a tight, mirthless laugh. "Funny when you think about it."

Vicky stood up, half-aware of the waitress standing at the next table, a plate balanced in each hand, her gaze fixed on them. The restaurant was silent. "You don't understand," she said, struggling to keep her voice under control. "There are people who want to destroy a sacred place. I can't turn away."

Lucas slammed his chair into the table, sending a little clatter through the dishes. She saw the muscles popping out of his clenched jaw as he grabbed the gray jacket hanging beside her raincoat and threw open the door. She watched him pass by the window, head and shoulders thrust forward, and she knew he would not stay at the house tonight.

"I can't, Lucas," she said after him.

She lifted her bag from the floor and dug her fingers into the leather to stop her hands from trembling. Finally she found her wallet and threw some bills on the table. They fluttered over the white napkin Lucas had tossed down. Without looking around at the eyes swimming toward her, she took her raincoat and went outside. The sidewalk was empty, a sheen of moisture on the pavement.

Vicky drove south on Federal Boulevard, in and out of the rain-blurred columns of light from the street lamps, feeling weak and shaky and chilled to the bone, as if she'd seen a specter of herself that she couldn't recognize. My God, what if Lucas was right? She was a junkie, living on danger. Ordinary life, normal things—weren't they enough? She would change, she told herself. She would give the information to Steve. He would inform the Fremont County sheriff in Lander and the officials on the res. Steve would arrest Nathan Baider for murder. That was his job. She could walk away.

She parked at the curb in front of her house and, holding her bag over her head in the rain, ran up the concrete steps. A gust of wind pulled at her raincoat and sent a spray of rain over the porch as she fumbled with the key.

She felt a deep chill run through her. Not from the argument with Lucas, not from the rain. It was a kind of cold that penetrated her soul. She had the sense that some invisible presence was watching her.

She whirled about. Nothing. The Bronco at the curb below, the passing cars with arrows of lights shooting into the darkness. Nothing except the rain in the trees and the sound of tires splashing on asphalt.

*Pay attention.* Her grandmother's voice. *Not everything is as it seems. Listen to the spirits. They will help you.*

She pushed the door open. The moment she stepped inside, she knew someone was there.

# ❖ 30 ❖

"Get up."

Father John heard the disembodied voice coming through the rain. The hard toe of a boot crashed against his ribs; pain exploded like thunder inside him. The smell of his own blood came at him in a warm rush. Grasping at the mud and rocks, he managed to maneuver to his knees. The thunder rumbled overhead, sending little tremors through the ground. For an instant the air was bright with lightning.

"I said get up." The boot thudded again.

Father John pushed himself upright against a boulder, the sharp edges digging into his back. Rain pounded on his shoulders, and his hair was matted against his head. He realized he'd lost his hat.

He blinked into the beam of a flashlight and tried to bring the surroundings into focus. He could make out the figure of a man almost as tall as he was in a black slicker with the hood pulled low. The jaw jutted forward, set in determination. He straddled the path, waving the flashlight up and down. In his other hand was a pistol that pointed at Father John's chest.

"What're you doin' up here?" he said.

An unfamiliar voice. Not a voice from the shadows of

the confessional. He was not someone he'd ever met, and yet Father John knew who he was. A man named Wentworth. *The meanest sonovabitch.*

"What've you done with Eddie and the girl?" he said through the pain. There was no sign of headlights in the trees below, only the rainy blackness. *Where are you, Slinger?*

The man dipped his head and moved in closer, like a boxer coming in for the knockout. Father John could see the moisture pooling in the jagged scar at the base of his jaw, as if someone had once tried to cut his throat.

"You're the priest put the article in the newspaper, aren't you?" He gave a sharp laugh. "You did Delaney and me a big favor. Eddie Ortiz came scurrying out of his hiding place, like a rat out of the fire."

Father John hunched over around the pain. He'd given Eddie away. Enticed him to the mission, and Wentworth and Delaney had been waiting. Eddie had probably led them to the girl. He felt his stomach churn.

Wentworth shone the flashlight up the narrow incline to the ledge; where another man stood, a slim figure in a red baseball jacket—the jacket he'd worn in the confessional. Delaney. Above the man, on the face of the cliff, was the white figure of the petroglyph.

"Where are they?" Father John managed, his voice tight with pain. The rain drummed on the boulders and careened off the face of the cliffs. The sounds of thunder drove the pain into his head and ribs.

"About to take a flying leap off a ledge." Wentworth gave a little laugh. "Suicide mission, I'd call it."

"Let them go," Father John said. He felt a wave of relief that Eddie and the girl were still alive. "They don't know anything about the diamond deposit here."

"Well, well." The pistol came closer, brushing his

jacket. "Sounds like you know more'n what's good for you. All the more reason for your speedy demise, Father O'Malley." He swung the flashlight around, casting a wavy beam over the sandstone cliff.

"Detective Slinger'll be here any minute," Father John said. Keep Wentworth talking. Delaney wasn't going to throw Eddie and the girl over on his own.

"You think I'm gonna believe that? The hick detective doesn't know his ass from a hole in the ground. Otherwise he'd be here now. I know about you Jesuits. Too smart for your own good. You figured things out and came up here on your own. Now you're going to die."

Wentworth stepped around, and Father John felt the pistol jam against his spine. "Get going," the man said, shining the flashlight up a narrow incline. "Don't make me shoot you here."

Father John started following the dim beam of light, conscious of the gun in the small of his back. His boots slid in the mud, and he had to dig the heels in hard to maintain his balance. The incline narrowed to no wider than a couple of feet. He edged along the cliff, keeping his hand on the sandstone for balance. A few steps and he was at another boulder field directly below the ledge. A faint light was shining above.

"Keep going." Wentworth pushed the gun in hard, and Father John started climbing. He felt as if spurs were cutting into his sides. The man was huffing behind him. Thunder roared again, followed by a white flash of lightning that made the boulders leap out, dark and shiny in the rain. He made it to the top and managed to haul himself onto the ledge. A bright light shone in his face.

"Why'd you come here, Father?" The voice in the confessional.

Father John knocked the flashlight aside. For an instant

he couldn't see anything, except the blue-and-yellow lights fizzing in his eyes. He blinked hard, trying to bring into focus the figure in the red jacket. Light hair and hooded eyes, pale, sunken cheeks, bulbous nose. He had the lanky frame, alert stance, and pent-up energy of a runner, as if were about to sprint off the ledge. The jacket shone in the light.

"Where are they?" Father John said. The ledge was a mosaic of rain and shadows. He was aware of Wentworth climbing up beside him, taking in loud gulps of air—a man out of shape, Father John thought. Wentworth hurled himself upright and set the flashlight next to the cliff. A thin stream of light washed over the petroglyph.

Father John felt the gun jabbing at his back again as the man in the red jacket shone his flashlight over the prone figures of Eddie Ortiz and Ali Burris, sprawled at the base of the cliff about ten feet away.

Father John could see the picture clearly now, like a video unrolling in front of him: Wentworth and Delaney forcing Eddie and the girl up the mud-slicked path, guns in their backs. Knocking them unconscious on the ledge. And then—two bodies would fly over the ledge, crash through the boulders, drop down the face of the cliff, breaking and flying apart. The injuries so extensive no pathologist would detect the initial blow to their skulls. Just like Duncan Grover.

He walked across the ledge, dropped down on one knee next to the girl, and took her hand. It was as light and cool as a leaf. He probed for a pulse—some sign of life. There it was, the faintest murmuring of blood beneath the skin in the soft underside of her wrist.

"Hang on, Ali," he said, hoping that his voice might seep into the girl's unconsciousness. He started to turn toward the motionless body of Eddie.

"Get away!" Wentworth shouted behind him.

A boot slammed into his shoulder, knocking him off balance. He felt himself sliding sideways across the wet sandstone, the ledge falling away. He grabbed at the surface, dug into the sandstone with his boots. Slowing himself finally. Stopping. He was at the edge, pain ripping through him. He could feel the abyss opening below.

Lightning zigzagged through the air, and the piñons and junipers stood out in the light a half second before dissolving back into the darkness. There was another crash of thunder. As he started inching away from the edge, he saw the faintest trace of light below, like an electrical charge.

He managed to get onto his hands and knees and crawl backward a few feet. Then he tried to stand up, crouching with the pain that circled his shoulders and rib cage and coursed down his spine. The rain came harder. He wiped the moisture from his eyes.

Wentworth was still standing next to Eddie and the girl. The pistol gleamed in the flashlight beam. The man in the red jacket stood a few feet away.

"Don't do this, Delaney," Father John said. "Think of your soul, man. Your immortal soul. You're putting yourself into hell."

"Shut up." Wentworth waved the pistol at him.

"How d'ya know my name?" Raw panic infused Delaney's voice.

"Detective Slinger knows you've been working a diamond deposit. He knows what happened to Duncan Grover. There's going to be a lot of policemen here in a few minutes."

"He's lying," Wentworth said.

"Jesus, Buck." Fear mingled with the panic in the other man's voice. "Baider'll kill us."

"He's bluffing, you damn fool."

"I didn't want no part of murder, Father." Delaney moved forward, holding out the flashlight in a kind of offering.

"Shut up, you fool." Wentworth swung the pistol toward the other man.

"Baider's using you," Father John said. "How many more people are you going to kill for him?"

The flashlight jumped in Delaney's hand, tossing light over Wentworth and the still bodies of Ali Burris and Eddie Ortiz. Father John realized something was different about Eddie: the hands curled into fists. The Indian was conscious.

"You got it all wrong, Father," Delaney said. "The boss says we take care of this last job—"

"Baider's lying." Father John tried to straighten his shoulders. He coughed, and for a half second his muscles froze with pain. The bitter taste of blood was in his mouth. An image of Vicky flashed in his mind. Alone in Denver, determined to find out what Baider Industries didn't want her to know. She would follow every lead, probe and probe, until, finally, she came face-to-face with a man who had people killed.

He took in a short breath, then another. "Wake up, Delaney," he managed. "Baider'll keep using you and Wentworth here to do his dirty work. Wentworth's too dumb to understand. You've got to save yourself, your own soul."

"Shut up, you damned priest." Wentworth lunged forward. The pistol crashed against Father John's ribs.

He doubled over. His rib cage had sprung apart; his lungs filled with acid.

"Let's get this show on the road." Wentworth was coming at him again, swinging the pistol overhead like a sledgehammer.

Father John dodged to the side as the metal slammed into the cliff. Clenching his fists, he went for the man, jabbing at the stomach beneath the slicker. The man pedaled backward, then caught himself.

"I'll kill you!" he shouted, coming forward again, head down, like a bull. The lightning snapped overhead, outlining the rage in his eyes. He gripped the pistol in both hands.

Father John pulled his arms in close to his sides, fists still clenched. He had no breath; he was on fire with pain. The barrel of the pistol looked as large as a black tunnel coming toward him.

Suddenly Wentworth was scrabbling sideways, howling like a trapped animal. Delaney was riding his back, slamming a fist into the man's head, jerking his arm up, grabbing at the pistol. Shouting: "No more, Buck. No more." A flashlight skittered across the ledge, throwing crazy patterns of light around.

The crack of gunfire mingled with the sound of thunder as the two men moved toward the cliff, bulls locked in combat, stumbling over Ali's crumpled legs, nearly falling onto Eddie. Then they were grappling backward, propelled by the momentum and the force of their grunts and shouts.

Thunder came again; the sky was white with lightning. The men stopped struggling. Suspended on the edge: two figures outlined against the sky. Father John realized they were falling.

He dove toward them, grabbing at fistfuls of the plastic slicker, the red baseball jacket, his fingers digging for skin and bone—something to hold on to. Everything was blurred. The rain beat on his head and shoulders. Pain exploded inside him. He felt the slicker slide through one hand. Wentworth was falling over the edge, clawing at Delaney as he fell, grabbing on to the other man's legs.

Father John held on to Delaney's arm as hard as he could. He dug his boots into the sandstone trying to counter the force pulling the man down.

He could feel Delaney start to go.

A shadow moved at his side, and Eddie reached out and grabbed Delaney's other arm as the man dropped over the edge.

Suddenly Father John felt the pressure release, and Delaney was free. Wentworth had let go. A high-pitched scream rent the air for a terrible moment, then was lost in the sounds of the rain.

"Hold on!" he shouted. Eddie was still gripping the man's other arm, but Delaney was like deadweight dangling in space. Father John could feel the red jacket start to slip through his hands. Like a jolt, it came to him that Eddie had let go and that he and Delaney were going to fall together into the darkness.

And then: a tightness around his waist, arms squeezing his rib cage. The pain made him retch, but he was steady now. He had a good hold on Delaney.

"Grab onto the edge!" he shouted.

Slowly Delaney's free hand came up and grasped for a purchase. Finally the fingers wrapped around a jagged piece of sandstone.

"Get ready!" Father John shouted again. "We're going to pull you up!"

He was already pulling, praying Eddie would hold on. Delaney's body started to rise over the edge: the light matted hair, the red jacket scrunched under his arms. And then the man was on his belly, legs extended into the darkness. Father John managed another hard yank, then another, until Delaney was sprawled motionless across the ledge.

He dropped down on one knee. The pain hit him like a bolt of lightning. There was no air. Seconds passed. Finally his breath started again, hard and fast, each breath like an inhalation of fire. He could hear his heart pounding. The thunder boomed overhead, a cacophony of sound that shook the ledge. "Wentworth's dead," he heard himself say.

"Thunder killed him," Eddie said. He was standing at the edge looking down. "Thunder came and destroyed the evil."

Below, a light was moving through the darkness. There was no question now: the light was coming up the path. Father John felt a surge of relief. Slinger had gotten the message.

Delaney was sobbing beside him, a low, guttural noise. Father John laid a hand on the man's shoulders. "You're gonna be okay," he said. Then he crawled over to the girl. The ledge was wet and cold beneath his hands. He picked up the thin wrist and probed once more for a pulse.

"They hit her pretty hard," Eddie said behind him. "I thought they killed her."

Delaney's sobs rose into a long-sustained howl, like that of a wounded animal.

The pulse was there, faint but regular. "She's alive," Father John said.

"O'Malley. You up there?" Slinger's voice sounded fuzzy in the rain.

"We need help!" he shouted down at the light wavering below.

There were the sounds of boots scratching over wet rock, someone gasping for breath. A minute passed before Slinger hauled himself over the boulders and onto the ledge, shining a flashlight about. The light stopped on the girl. "Medic!" the detective shouted.

A couple of uniformed officers were coming up behind him. One of them bounded forward and went straight to the girl. He checked her throat and wrist, then shone a flashlight onto her face. She looked like a sleeping child, eyelids flickering a moment before she awoke.

"No!" she screamed. The small body began to shake, pulling back toward the cliff, as if she could disappear into the sandstone with the spirits.

Father John leaned closer. "It's okay, Ali. It's over." She stared up at him out of eyes wild with disbelief.

"Eddie?" she said finally.

"I'm here." The Indian moved between Father John and the medic and took the girl's hand.

"You want to tell me what the hell happened up here?" Slinger said.


"I need a phone, Slinger," Father John said.

The overhead light flickered inside the detective's cruiser. Outside was only the darkness and the rain pounding on the roof.

Slinger lifted his head from the notebook balanced on the steering wheel. He'd been scribbling for the last five minutes.

It had taken almost an hour to walk down the path. An officer leading the way, shining the flashlight ahead, then Eddie and Delaney and two officers carrying Ali in a tarp.

Father John had followed the tarp, every step sending shock waves through him. Slinger was beside him, grabbing his arm from time to time to steady him. He must've been stumbling, he realized. He felt weak and dizzy with pain.

On the way down he'd managed to tell the detective about the diamond deposit in the valley, about the boss in Denver—Baider—ordering Buck Wentworth and Jimmie Delaney to kill anyone who found out about the deposit, about the fight on the ledge and Wentworth's body somewhere below on the cliffs.

After the two officers had gotten Ali into the back of a van, the medic insisted on taking a closer look at him. He'd crawled into the van beside the girl. The soaked jacket came off, then the shirt that clung to his skin. Fingers probed at him. "Got a broken rib, maybe two," the medic announced. Finally the tape, tightening around him. Father John had groaned with the pain.

"You'll want to get an X-ray at the hospital . . ."

He had no intention of going to the hospital. He'd managed to get out of the van and stumble through the rain, past the sedan with Eddie and Delaney in the backseat, to another sedan where Slinger was bent over the notebook.

He'd crawled into the backseat. "I've got to warn Vicky Holden before—"

"Before what?"

"Before Baider kills her."

"Look, Father, we've got a team coming up to try and retrieve whatever's left of Wentworth's body. Soon's we wrap this up, we'll send an official report to the Denver police."

That's when he'd said he had to use the phone *now*.

The detective looked across the seat at him. "Take it easy, Father." He reached inside his raincoat and handed him a black cell phone.

Father John dialed Vicky's number at home. He could make out the numbers on the dashboard clock: eight-oh-five. She should be home. He concentrated on the electronic buzz of a phone ringing somewhere in Denver, barely aware of the tape digging into his skin. His own pain receded in the distance.

"Pick up," he said into the receiver. "For god's sake, pick up."

# ❖ 31 ❖

The sound of the phone startled her, erupting as it did out of the silence that enveloped the house. Vicky stood in the entry a moment, gripping the doorknob, staring into the shadows. No one was there, and yet something was different. She tried to make out what it might be. An unfamiliar odor. Aftershave? Perspiration?

The phone continued ringing.

She fumbled for the panel of light switches next to the door. The house burst into light: living room on the left; dining room straight ahead. She tried to shake off the feeling of uneasiness that clung to her like a fever.

Five, six rings now. Vicky crossed the dining room and picked up the cordless phone. Black letters floated into the green readout space: FREMONT COUNTY SHERIFF.

"Hello." Her voice sounded shaky.

A shadow moved. The phone jerked out of her hand and clattered on the floor. A muscular arm encircled her waist, a hand clamped over her mouth. She felt the pain rip across her shoulders as she spun around. Her head was jammed back into the rocklike muscles of a man's chest, her cheek buried against the fabric of a coat. Metal buttons pulled at her hair and dug into her scalp. She couldn't breathe.

She felt herself floating upward, watching a scene below: the woman—who was she? So small inside the man's grasp—struggling, arms flailing, head tilted back, eyes wide in disbelief and fear locked on the ceiling.

The hand moved away from her mouth and gripped her shoulder. She gasped with the pain. She couldn't breathe: where was the air? Her heart was bursting inside her chest. Finally she caught a breath, then another, and forced herself to relax. The man's grip loosened.

She waited for two heartbeats, and then, with all of her strength, she rammed her elbow back into the man's ribs. His hand came up to her face, a reflexive motion, and she bit hard into the fleshy palm.

"Bitch!" The voice sounded like thunder.

She was free. A bulky man in a black coat was pedaling backward. She stumbled against the telephone stand, knocking it to the floor, and started for the entry.

The blow came out of nowhere. She crashed against the wall, her legs melting beneath her. The shock gave way to an explosion of pain in her face. She tried to scream, but no sound would come.

The fist rose again, and she drew inward against the stuccoed wall, steeling herself for another blow.

"Enough." Another male voice sounded through the pain. "She won't be any good to us unconscious."

The man in the black raincoat still loomed above her, his breath coming in jagged bursts of air ripe with garlic and old cigarettes. She felt the pressure of his grip on her shoulders as he jerked her upright and propelled her past the dining-room table and into the living room. She stumbled out of her shoes, her feet in nylons skidding over the wood floor. She crashed against the coffee table and fell onto the sofa, the knobs of her spine bumping against the armrest.

The second man slipped past and dropped onto the coffee table. He smoothed the flaps of his raincoat over his thighs and gave her a long, tolerant smile.

She'd seen him before: in the entry to the Equitable Building the day she'd gone to see his father. She'd gotten it all wrong. She'd assumed Nathan Baider was still in charge of the company, that he'd had Vince Lewis killed to keep the diamond deposit secret. But it was his son, Roz. Roz who'd been having an affair with Jana Lewis. Roz was the one Jana had confronted about her husband's murder, and he'd had her killed, too.

Roz Baider leaned toward her. "My apologies, Ms. Holden," he said. He adjusted the flaps of his raincoat again around his gray suit pants.

"Get out," she managed through the pain.

He gave her a benign smile, the kind he might bestow on a naughty child. "We're all reasonable people here." He glanced up at the large man moving like a black shadow above his shoulder. "Allow me to introduce Kurt, my security chief, who, incidentally, never saw a lock he couldn't pick. I'm afraid your lock posed no challenge whatsoever."

Vicky shifted her gaze to the man in the black raincoat. He'd been with Roz at the Equitable Building, but she'd seen him somewhere else: in the black sedan passing her on I-25. As she stared at him, his features rearranged themselves into a satisfied grin.

"Kurt may get a little overzealous at times," Roz Baider said. "Unfortunately there's been some necessary violence . . ." Another shrug. "There's no need for more, I'm sure you agree. I see no reason that we can't come to an amicable understanding."

Vicky took in several breaths. Her mind was focused

into a pinprick of clarity. *Be thoughtful.* Survival depended upon it.

"Tell me something," she said. She was thinking, Keep them talking. Death could come in the silences. "What makes you think you can mine diamonds at Bear Lake? It's a sacred place. Surely you know that. It's been sacred to my people for centuries, longer than anyone can remember. You'll never get permission to mine there."

"You think I want to operate mines the rest of my life?" A note of incredulity sounded in Baider's tone. "My dear woman, I have no such intention."

She stared at him. How could she have gotten it wrong? She'd seen the satellite image, she had the evidence.

"I know where the kimberlite pipe is located," she said. Her head and shoulders throbbed.

"Of course you do. You've been a busy little bee, running up to Laramie this morning to talk to Charlie Ferguson, going to Global Vision this afternoon."

The image of the black sedan flashed again in her mind. Following her to Laramie, shooting past on I-25 this evening, Kurt's face averted. She understood. He'd taken the Speer exit before she'd reached it and he'd come here. The sedan was probably in the alley. At what point had he called Roz? "I've got her. She's on the way home. We'll have a little surprise party waiting."

"The diamond world's a very small place," Roz Baider was saying. "Soon as you left Ferguson's office, he called my father—they're colleagues, you see. He wanted to know if we'd stumbled on a pipe at Bear Lake. Very unfortunate." He shook his head. "Alarmed the old man for no reason. Caused somewhat of a problem at the office, I'm afraid. I have no time for problems."

"Your father doesn't know about the deposit, does he?"

Vicky said, her mind still grappling with this new image of what was going on.

Baider leaned toward hcr, thc narrowed eyes as opaque as stone. "My father prefers to concentrate his energies on golf. In any case, he no longer understands the diamond world. With rebels taking over the mines in Africa, the rush is on to develop new mines. Naturally the major diamond companies are eager to find deposits in the United States. The Loesseur Group, for example. Perhaps you've heard of them? No? Major competitor for De-Beers. Loesseur has agreed to buy Baider Industries, after a great deal of effort on my part, let me add."

He paused and ran his tongue over his thin lips. "Let's just say that Loesseur lost interest for a while, after one of our mines played out, but as soon as they heard about the rich deposit we'd located at Bear Lake, they changed their minds. They're eager to extend their operations into this region."

"You can't sell what you don't own, Baider." Vicky made her voice strong. "You don't have a mineral lease on the area. You don't have any authorization to explore."

"True, true." Roz Baider nodded for a long moment. "We're selling information, my dear. Information about a rich deposit. Loesseur will take care of the legal technicalities and begin operations."

Vicky felt a chill run through her. A company that competed with DeBeers, with deep pockets to pay for the environmental study required for a mining permit and fleets of top-notch lawyers, would be able to withstand any challenges the tribes might offer. She said, "A mine will destroy the Bear Lake Valley."

Roz Baider was grinning at some image in his head. "I can assure you that Loesseur will not operate a mine long."

"You talk too much, Roz." Kurt stepped forward, the massive body throwing a shadow over the other man.

"What are you saying?" Vicky kept her eyes on the man perched in front of her. "Loesseur wouldn't buy your company if they didn't intend to operate a mine."

"Oh, they have every intention of operating a mine. Our tests prove conclusively that the diamonds at Bear Lake are gem quality. Yes, yes, the very best, worth millions." He slapped one hand against his thigh. "By the time Loesseur gets results from their own tests, I'll be in Brazil. Kurt here—" He glanced up at the man glaring at him. "Where will you be, Kurt? Switzerland?"

"Shut up, Roz."

Vicky glanced from Baider to Kurt. An old story, a legend she'd heard as a kid, flitted at the edge of her mind. The con artists in the Wyoming wilderness a century ago, duping the big-money boys in New York City by making them believe there were gem-quality diamonds in a deposit, when the only gems found were the ones they had sprinkled around.

"You salted the deposit," she said.

Roz Baider threw his head back and laughed, then ran a hand under his eyes and dabbed at the moisture. "Funny, isn't it?" he said. "Company out west scamming an international diamond company. By the time Loesseur's geologists figure it out, the deal will be closed and I'll have twenty million dollars in an account in Brazil."

"Shut up, you damn fool." Kurt took hold of Baider's shoulder and pushed him down onto the table. "You've got a big mouth."

Baider pulled himself free and sat back up, rubbing at his shoulder, an aggrieved look in his eyes. "What difference does it make? She's not going to be around to tell anybody."

Vicky slid down the sofa, trying to put as much space between herself and the two men as she could. A chill had taken hold of her, as if a cold wind had swept through the house. There were no sounds of any other humans— no cars passing outside, no phone ringing. She was alone with the men.

*Keep talking.* "You killed Vince Lewis." She locked eyes with the man in the black raincoat. "Roz gave the order, and you drove the sedan. Vince was going to blow the whistle, wasn't he? Why? Did the man have a conscience?"

Roz Baider gave a nervous laugh. He was still rubbing his shoulder. "Lewis didn't like it I was screwing his wife, despite the fact he was screwing half the women on Seventeenth Street. He thought if he ruined me, Jana wouldn't want me. She wouldn't divorce him and throw him out of the mansion. He could keep his rich man's life. The bastard would have blown the whole deal out of the water. Fortunately I overheard him making an appointment with you on the telephone. I knew what he intended to do, and I couldn't let him do it, now could I?"

"Why did you kill Jana?" Vicky glanced at the man in the raincoat. "She couldn't have done any harm. She didn't have any evidence."

Kurt reared back. "You got it wrong, sweetheart. The lady's sudden demise wasn't my doing." He gestured to Baider, still rubbing at his shoulder.

"An unfortunate accident." Baider turned his gaze on some point above the sofa. "Jana was a very silly, stupid woman. She asked too many questions, got hysterical over what happened to her husband. Said she didn't want anything to do with murder. The woman should have been thanking me." He shrugged. "You never know about a lush."

Vicky felt like she was going to be sick. The man perched across from her had beaten Jana Lewis to death. Had he dumped her body? Or had he called in Kurt to mop up after him?

"Enough stalling!" Kurt shot forward, and Vicky felt herself being lifted off the sofa, his fingers digging into her bones, shooting pain through her body.

"You have information we want," he shouted. "We can make this easy, or we can make it hard. You cooperate, or you're going to be in more pain than you could ever imagine. Do you understand?"

Vicky tried to wrench herself away, but his grip tightened. The man's face came close to hers: lips peeled back from clenched teeth. "Who have you talked to beside Ferguson and the scientist at Global Vision? Who else knows about the deposit?"

"Everyone," she said. The pain pulsating through her body seemed remote and unimportant. All of her energies were concentrated now on staying alive. "Detective Clark. He's on his way over now."

"You're lying." The sharp, open-palmed blow across her face sent her spinning backward onto the sofa.

"He's already talked to the sheriff in Lander," she managed. She could taste the blood in her mouth. "That was the sheriff on the phone wanting more information."

The house went quiet. Kurt seemed to hold his breath for a long moment. Then: "Check the phone, Roz."

Roz lifted himself from the coffee table and disappeared into the dining room. Vicky was aware of his footsteps clacking across the wood floor, and something else: the almost imperceptible sound of a door opening. Cool air floated over the room.

Baider was back, his gaze on the receiver in his hand. "She's right. This says Fremont County Sheriff."

"Let's get her out of here."

Vicky leaned away, but Kurt had hold of her again, lifting her upright. She let her weight go dead, and the man pulled her across the coffee table. She felt the table edge cut into her shinbone.

"Nobody's going anywhere." The voice boomed from the entry, and Vicky jerked back onto the sofa. Past Kurt, past Roz, she could see Nathan Baider standing in the archway: He was all in gray: gray overcoat hanging open over a gray suit, thin strands of gray hair combed back from a gray face.

"What have you done?" The man kept his eyes on his son.

"Dad! Stay out of this."

The older man remained motionless, never taking his eyes away. "You lied to me. You said there was nothing in what this lady told Charlie Ferguson. I decided to come over here and talk to her myself. And what do I find? My own son—"

Suddenly, like a rattler striking out, Nathan Baider sprang across the room and began pushing his son backward. "You think I don't know about the kimberlite pipe at Bear Lake?" Pushing. Shouting. The phone thudded on the floor. "I found that pipe forty years ago and kept it secret all this time. Bear Lake is holy, you fool. You think I wanted some bozo up there desecrating a sacred place?"

Vicky had the sense of watching a film fast-forwarding: Roz rolling backward into the dining room, the old man's fists crashing into his face and chest, pummeling his stomach. "You ruined my name. Ruined the company I spent my life building."

"You crazy son of a bitch." Kurt lunged after them and threw his weight against the old man, who stumbled sideways, fists flailing in the air. Kurt's hand shot out, his palm sliced at the man's neck, and, in slow motion now, Nathan Baider began falling forward, dropping onto his hands and knees, collapsing at his son's feet. Kurt raised his hand again, but Roz grabbed hold of it and wrenched it to the man's back. "My father! Stop, you idiot! He's my father!"

Vicky was on her feet, darting around the coffee table. She scooped up the telephone as she ran, aware of Kurt pulling free and starting after her. She was through the entry, out the door, across the porch—running down the cement walk, rain slapping at her face, fingers groping for the 911 keys, scarcely aware of the shadowy figure coming up the steps until she had run into him.

"Vicky. Vicky. What is it?"

She stared up at Steve Clark, trying to make out if he was real or only a vision conjured up out of her own need. She'd prayed for help, and a spirit had arrived.

She grasped the smooth, moist fabric of his raincoat and pressed against his chest. She could feel his heart pounding. He *was* real.

"They're inside!" she heard herself scream.

"What happened?"

"Nathan Baider. I think they killed him."

Beyond Steve, coming up the steps, were two officers. They stopped on either side of them, and Vicky could sense the coiled energy beneath the dark uniforms.

"Who else is inside?" Steve's voice.

"Roz and his security chief, Kurt. I think Nathan—"

"Stay here," Steve cut in. He brushed past her, pulling out a small black pistol from beneath his sport coat, issuing orders to the officers. "Johnson around back. Adler, you and I go in front."

Vicky sank onto a small boulder in the flower garden next to the sidewalk and lifted her face into the rain and thanked the spirits.

# ◀ 32 ▶

The quiet awakened her. Even the drumming of rain against the roof had stopped. Vicky stretched against the rough fabric of the sofa in the study upstairs and winced at the pain that stabbed at her head and chest. She adjusted the ice pack on her cheek and glanced at the clock on the table next to the phone. The green numerals floated in the shadows: one-thirty.

She'd dozed for almost an hour. It surprised her. She hadn't expected to fall asleep; she'd still felt coiled for flight when Steve had led her upstairs. When did the noises downstairs stop? The footsteps scuffing the floor; the buzz of voices, the squawk of a police radio?

She listened to the silence, wondering if the officers and technicians had left. After a few moments she heard the footsteps on the carpeted stairs, followed by a soft knock. The door swung open, and Steve Clark stood in the opening. "You awake?" he said softly.

"Come in."

He stepped into the room and stood looking down at her, like a hesitant visitor to a hospital room, unsure if the patient was still alive. Finally he reached around, pulled the desk chair over, and sat down. "How are you feeling?"

"I'll be okay."

He was quiet a moment. "The techs have pretty much finished up downstairs," he said finally. "Just got word from the emergency room. Looks like Nathan will recover."

Vicky closed her eyes a moment. She found that she was shaking with relief. The image of the man in the black raincoat karate-chopping the old man's neck, was burned into her retinas. "He saved my life," she said. "If he hadn't come when he did—"

"I know." He placed a hand over hers. Outside, a car splashed through the wetness.

"I've spoken with Detective Slinger up in Lander. He'll be here tomorrow to interview Roz and Kurt. I expect we'll have enough evidence to charge them with masterminding the murder at Bear Lake, as well as the murders of Vince and Jana Lewis. Not to mention charges of conspiracy, kidnapping, assault, and attempted murder." He drew in a long, considered breath and exhaled slowly. "I'll need a full statement from you tomorrow." He glanced at his watch. "Make that this afternoon."

She'd already told him everything. After the officers had taken Roz and Kurt out the front door, hands cuffed behind their backs, and the ambulance had driven off with Nathan Baider, and the medics had handed her an ice pack, she'd sat at the dining-room table across from Steve, pouring out a torrent of words, as if the words could dispel the terror and pain. Why had he come when he did? she'd asked him.

Her friend had called, he'd explained. Father O'Malley. Said to get to the house. A killer could be there. He'd had the dispatcher send a car, and he'd come as fast as he could.

Now he said, "You shouldn't be alone, Vicky. Why isn't Lucas here? I'll call him for you."

"No." She shook her head.

"He's your son. He should be with you."

"I don't want to upset him." She drew in a breath. "I'll talk to him later."

He didn't say anything for a moment. "Is there someone else I can call. A friend?"

She pressed the ice pack into her face. Laola, a young woman with next Saturday's date the most serious thing on her mind; colleagues at the law firm—she didn't even have their home numbers; a couple of neighbors with whom she exchanged good mornings. There was no one. She was alone. *Hisei ci nihi.*

He said, "I can stay downstairs if you like."

"I'll be okay," she told him with as much confidence as she could muster. "Thanks."

He sighed and got to his feet. "I'll lock up on my way out," he said. Then: "By the way, I hung up the phone downstairs. It's working now."

The phone. She'd run outside with it, trying to dial 911, and then she'd bumped into Steve. She vaguely remembered setting the phone down somewhere—the dining-room table?—after Steve had brought her back into the house. She must have left it turned on. Anyone trying to call would have gotten a busy signal.

"Call me if you need me," he said, heading into the hallway. She heard his footsteps pounding on the stairs. After a moment the muffled thud of the front door shutting.

She started to get up, then dropped back. The room whirled about, and her head throbbed. She'd spend the night on the sofa, she decided. As she reached for the throw at the end, the phone rang. She leaned over to the table and lifted the receiver.

"Vicky. Thank God." John O'Malley's voice. She knew it instantly. "I've been trying to reach you all night. Are you okay?"

She curled up against the back cushion and allowed the comfort of his voice to wash over her. "Steve got here in time," she heard herself explaining. "I'm all right." She pushed away the memory of the blows and hurried on, telling him how Nathan Baider had walked in, like a spirit suddenly appearing out of nowhere, and how she had run out of the house.

The line went quiet a moment. "One of Baider's men died tonight at Bear Lake," he said. He told her about Wentworth and Delaney, how Delaney had broken down and told the detective everything. How Wentworth had spotted Grover at Bear Lake, the Indian who had worked for him at the Kimberly Mine. He'd assumed Grover had found out about the deposit somehow and had come to Bear Lake to spy on them, intending to blackmail Baider Industries or blow the whistle. He went up to the ledge to kill him. Delaney had gone along, but he hadn't expected Wentworth to kill the Indian.

Vicky tried to follow what he was saying through the throbbing in her head. Nothing was making sense. "Grover was on a vision quest," she managed.

That was right, he said. "The irony is, Grover didn't know anything about the deposit. Neither did Eddie, but when Wentworth spotted Eddie in Lander, he figured Grover and Eddie were working together. Eddie also had to die. They went after him. When they picked him up this afternoon, the guy was so scared he told them Ali Burris knew they'd killed Grover and was going to tell the sheriff, so they picked her up, too."

Vicky didn't say anything for a moment. It made sense now, the picture was clear. She uncurled her legs and set her bare feet on the carpet. "There's another irony," she said. "There won't be a mine at Bear Lake after all."

"I know," he said. "Delaney told Slinger how he and Wentworth had salted the mine. They sent Baider soil samples that included gem-quality stones, which Baider used to prove that the deposit was valuable. He was determined that his scheme would succeed, Vicky. He was willing to have people killed. He would have had you killed."

"You, too, John O'Malley," she said. Then she got up and walked over to the window, still feeling shaky. Outside, a section of pavement shimmered like a diamond under the street lamp. But it wasn't a diamond. Was nothing as it seemed? Everything an image of something else?

"I'd like to see the kimberlite pipe," she said.

"I have a good idea where it's located."

"Well, I know the exact location. And . . ." She drew in a long breath. A car broke through the diamond of light. "I want to come home."

# ‹ 33 ›

Father John saw Vicky standing next to the Bronco by the clump of willows. She was peering up through a pair of binoculars, seemingly lost in another reality. He turned into the parking area and stopped a few feet away.

It had been six weeks since the night they'd talked. Six weeks, and his ribs were still sore. Her call this morning had caught him by surprise. He knew she'd come home for a visit, but he didn't know when.

"I'm here for the weekend," she'd said, lightness and anticipation in her voice. "How about a hike in Bear Lake Valley this afternoon?"

Not until he got out of the Toyota and slammed the door did she seem to realize he was there. She took the binoculars away and walked toward him. She resembled the image of her he carried in his mind: dressed in blue jeans and a jean jacket, unbuttoned over a white T-shirt. Her black hair trailed around the collar. A red backpack dangled on her back. Her beaded earrings shimmered in the sunlight as she moved. There was a flush of color in her cheeks, a hint of red in her lips.

She handed him the binoculars and nodded toward the ledge where he'd gone after Eddie and Ali. "Look up there," she said, as if they'd been having an ongoing conversation.

He lifted the binoculars and focused beyond the lakeshore, moving slowly up the mountainside. The petroglyph leaped out at him: white arms, hands, and feet, the masked face, the round eyes. An otherworldly figure—spiritual—floating in space, so close he could almost reach out and touch it.

"Beautiful, isn't it?" Vicky said beside him.

"Yes."

After a moment she said, "Look this way." He felt the cool touch of her hand on his, guiding the binoculars toward another petroglyph, another spirit. "They'll leave here, you know, if the land is disturbed."

He understood. The spirits had been sent here by the Creator to help human beings and, when necessary, to chastise them.

He found another petroglyph, smaller, with deeply chiseled eyes and an upturned mouth that gave the face an amused expression. Spirits manifesting themselves in stone? It defied scientific theory and all the Jesuit logic he had absorbed through the years, both of which seemed inadequate to account for the reality. He believed in spirits. He believed in angels and saints. He believed in sacred places where the Creator was close, very close. Often he felt an unworldly presence at St. Francis.

He took the binoculars away and turned to Vicky. She was studying a small black box in her hand.

"GPS," she said. "The data analyst who found the pipe insisted I bring this along. He loaded the coordinates. All we have to do is follow the directions. A satellite up there somewhere"—she glanced at the sky—"will take us to the pipe."

She started walking, glancing now and then at the GPS

in her hand. He stayed in step beside her. The wild grasses and brush spreading across the valley were dappled in sunlight. Clouds as white as snow billowed over the mountain peaks.

They headed in a slightly different direction than he would have chosen. He'd seen the movement when he'd first gone to the ledge. He was pretty sure he could find the pipe without the gadget, but it was probably taking them by the most direct route.

"I'll be moving back," Vicky said. She kept her eyes straight ahead.

"When?" He wasn't surprised. The moccasin telegraph had been weighted down with rumors: she was moving this weekend, next weekend, next year.

"Next month." She stopped walking and looked around, taking into herself the mountains and cliffs, the creeks meandering through the valley to the lake. "This is mine," she said.

"What about Lucas?"

"He's all for it. We've had long talks, he and I. He thinks I'll be safer here, where his father is." She gave a little laugh and started out again.

Father John walked alongside her without saying anything. He knew she'd gone to Denver to get away from Ben Holden. He wondered where he'd be next month. At St. Francis, he hoped, but he could never be certain. He was on borrowed time here. Every day precious, to be enjoyed while it lasted.

"I have some business to finish up at the firm," Vicky went on. She swung her backpack around, removed a bottle of water, and took a long drink. Then she handed the bottle to him. Her lipstick on the rim had a sweet taste. "But now that the appellate court has overturned the ruling in the Navajo Nation case . . ."

"Congratulations," he said. He'd read about the ruling in the *Gazette* a week ago.

She gave him a smile that betrayed her satisfaction. "Anyway," she went on, "the firm doesn't have any other important cases affecting Indian people at the moment. A good time to come home."

She drew in a long breath. "Even after I get back, I'll have to return to Denver to testify at the trials of Baider and Kurt. They're looking at the death penalty, and that's before Wyoming gets a shot at them."

Father John didn't say anything for a moment. He was thinking of Jimmie Delaney. He'd visited the man yesterday. Shrunken with remorse against the cement wall of a cell at the county jail in Lander, he'd pleaded guilty to accessory to murder, conspiracy, assault. After he testified against his bosses, he'd probably be sentenced to a long prison term.

They were headed up an incline now, and Father John felt the same pull in his calves he'd felt running up the mountain to the ledge. It had been raining then and dark. Now the sun burned warm through the shoulders of his jacket, despite the clouds building over the mountains. In the distance, he could hear the faintest rumble of thunder, sputtering like an engine trying to turn over. It would rain later.

Vicky dropped down on a boulder and took another drink. A little row of perspiration glistened on her forehead, just below her hairline. He sat next to her and took a drink after she'd finished.

"What about the lawsuit?" she said.

He took a moment before answering. "We're going to settle with the woman."

"What?" Vicky turned toward him. "She followed Father Ryan here. That hardly makes her an innocent party. You might have won in court."

"So the lawyers say."

"Well, who suggested settling?" She stared at him a moment. "Why?"

Father John shrugged. "The man made promises he couldn't keep. She believed him, gave up her job, moved to Riverton. It'll take her a while to get over it." He held her gaze a moment. "A man shouldn't do that to a woman," he said.

"Oh, John." She shook her head. "Some developer will put up a box store on the land and cover the earth with an asphalt parking lot."

"Maybe not," he said. "The Provincial's trying to convince a wealthy benefactor to buy the land and donate it back to the mission."

"You have the luck of the Irish, John O'Malley."

"Yes," he said. "And usually it's—"

"Well, let's hope this time it'll be good." She stood up. "The GPS says we have another couple miles. We'd better get going before it rains."

He followed her up another incline. On the far side, he could see the parallel tracks of flattened grasses and scrub brush. The tracks wound to the left, but Vicky continued straight ahead: the direct route, guided by an invisible satellite.

They were in a wide meadow now, mountains curving around the far side. Vicky stopped and studied the GPS a moment, then walked past a grove of willows and stopped again. He followed.

Erupting through the grass and brush, barely visible, was a large circle of gray-black rocks. In the center, a slight depression where the earth had a bluish cast.

Father John stooped down and picked up a rock the

size of his hand. He turned it over, testing the weight and heft. It looked like hardened lava. "Hard to believe diamonds make their home in such simple rock," he said. Like the spirits, he was thinking, in the sandstone cliffs.

Vicky started walking again, holding out the GPS. He went after her. "Baider's crew was digging here." She gestured toward a small area. The earth had been tamped down, and clusters of wild grasses struggled to get a foothold, unlike the grass flourishing nearby.

"Looks as if Gus Iron Bear and the other elders had the damage repaired," he said.

Vicky stooped over and brushed at the stand of new grass. It sprang up under her hand. She stood up and turned toward him. "Maybe the spirits repaired the damage. This is their home."

She smiled and went on: "What if the spirits played a trick on Baider and his crew? What if the spirits salted the area?"

He held her eyes. "You mean, put the lesser-quality diamonds near the surface where they'd find them and hid the gem-quality stones far below?"

"Well, Father O'Malley," she said, "what does your Jesuit logic say to that?"

"It says we don't know everything."

She started laughing, and the sound of her laughter mingled with the first clap of thunder over the mountaintops, like the pounding of horses' hooves far away, drawing closer.

He said, "Jesuit logic also says it's going to rain."

She shook her head. "It's only thunder guarding this place."

"All the same, we'd better start back."

"We're walking softly here," she said, taking his arm as they started back across the meadow, retracing their steps. "We don't have anything to fear. Thunder won't harm us."